SO-EKM-858

HEAVEN WHERE
THE BACHELORS SIT

Gerard Windsor was born in Sydney in 1944. He spent
seven years as a Jesuit, but left before ordination. He
later obtained degrees from the Australian National
University and Sydney University. He has published
two collections of short stories, a novella and a
collection of autobiographical stories. His short stories,
articles and reviews have appeared in numerous
anthologies, literary magazines and newspapers. He
lives in Sydney with his wife and son.

Other books by Gerard Windsor

The Harlots Enter First
Memories of the Assassination Attempt
That Fierce Virgin
Family Lore

GERARD WINDSOR

HEAVEN WHERE THE BACHELORS SIT

University of Queensland Press

First published 1996 by University of Queensland Press
Box 42, St Lucia, Queensland 4067 Australia

© Gerard Windsor 1996

This book is copyright. Apart from any fair dealing
for the purposes of private study, research, criticism
or review, as permitted under the Copyright Act, no
part may be reproduced by any process without written
permission. Enquiries should be made to the publisher.

Typeset by University of Queensland Press
Printed in Australia by McPherson's Printing Group

Distributed in the USA and Canada by
International Specialized Book Services, Inc.,
5804 N.E. Hassalo Street, Portland, Oregon 97213–3640

 This project has been assisted by
the Commonwealth Government through
the Australia Council, its arts funding
and advisory body.

Cataloguing in Publication Data
National Library of Australia

Windsor, Gerard, 1944–   .
  Heaven where the bachelors sit.

  1. Windsor, Gerard, 1944–   . 2. Jesuits — Australia —
  Biography. 3. Authors, Australian — 20th century —
  Biography. 4. Ex-priests, Catholic — Australia — Biography.
  I. Title.

A823.3

ISBN 0 7022 2910 5

*For Michael McKernan
and all at Watsonia*

Several parts of this book, in a different form, appeared in the *Adelaide Review, Eureka Street, Southerly*, the *Sydney Morning Herald*, and *Voices*.

I have received generous and unconditional help from many people, especially John Cowburn S.J., Tom Daly S.J., Rosanne Fitzgibbons, Charles Fraser S.J., Morag Fraser, Peter Kelly, Margaret Kennedy, Peter L'Estrange S.J., Michael McKernan, John Parker, Christopher Pearson, Robert Schneider, Paul Schulze S.J., Lyn Tranter and Caroline Walsh. My thanks to them all.

Contents

If a Son Asks for Bread   1

Summer 1963   4

Raising the Mind and Heart   8

On the Society's Terms   17

Our Conversation Is in Heaven   29

Over the Hills and Far Away   47

I Preach, But Not Myself   56

The Light of the Shadow of Death   64

The Lifeless Bodies of Great-Souled Heroes   72

All Things Being Done to Edify   84

Making Ourselves Eunuchs   97

I Applied My Heart to Wisdom   110

The Drama in Our Lives   121

Dick Hall's Fable   133

Scattered Leaves: A Spoiled Priest   161

Scattered Leaves: A Biography for Michael Scott   168

Scattered Leaves: My Mother's House   183

The Blood of Christ   193

If a Son Asks for Bread

Matthew 7.9

When I got to school I opened my satchel to take out my pencils and exercise book, and I saw there was no lunch. Nowhere. The satchel had no hidden compartments. There was no lunch. The absence horrified me. I was five, and I gaped, stock-still, on the edge of this blank. I had never not had a lunch before. The lunch was there, like the tram to school, like the bells sending the same orders to us all. But where the lunch should be there was just an empty, stale space. All through the morning I could feel the emptiness.

When the bell finally rang for the end of class boys streamed from the room and I was spun with them. When they crowded around the wall hooks in the dark gloom below the stairs and began to unlace their satchels and click open their Globites I stood back.

I never thought of doing without lunch. Lunch had to happen. It would not be what it should be, it would not be what my mother provided. But there had to be something. There was no adult with us; they had gone to their own lunch, or they were waiting in the playground. Other boys jogged past me, prising the lid from a tin, pocketing a piece of fruit, crying to one another to wait.

I stepped aside and then turned my back and pushed open the door into the silent, out-of-bounds assembly hall. I waited for a query or a summons but there was no one there. I sped past the windows that looked into the courtyard, slipped into the carpeted entrance hall coming in off the archway and pushed on under the grand staircase to the headmaster's study. I moved towards the half circle of light from the northern sun that flooded through the bay windows on to the desk at the far end. Colours flared and sparkled all around me. The room was hung with paintings. Other framed canvases stood stacked, faces out, against the walls. I saw the Christ Child and the Wise Men. Lean, sharp-lined figures brought their bold, unsustaining gifts to the baby. Gold for the king, incense for the god, myrrh for the man who is to die.

Father Scott was behind his desk, writing. A grave, bespectacled, heavy-eyebrowed man, but with the points of a smile, an adult smile, warm but also withheld, flickering in his eyes.

"What can we do for you, Threepence?" he said. I had a younger sister, Penny, so I was Threepence.

"I forgot my lunch, Father," I said. He was a priest, and I knew it was a confession as much as a request for help. I had no idea what the consequences of such a mistake were.

"Ah, you don't know the routine, I suppose," he said. He recapped his pen and stood up, his smile filling out a little more, but a smile still only just in the ascendant over a frown. "We'd better see Edie." Briefly he rested his hand behind my shoulders and steered me down a corridor, past a room where other Jesuits were already settling at table, to a kitchen whose need here had hardly occurred to me. A middle-aged Italian couple sat at a wooden table in the corner, dressed in work clothes and eating with their fingers.

"Good day, Nando," said Father Scott. "Edie, this is Threepence. He's forgotten his lunch. Would you be able to do him something?"

Still chewing, Edie worked her buttocks across her chair and walked over to the central table, slapping her hands on her apron. "Sandwich?" she asked.

"Yes, please." I was relieved that it didn't have to be anything more unusual.

Father Scott was gone. Edie took up a flat-bottomed but

otherwise oval loaf such as I had never seen before and sheared two large chunks from it. "One sandwich? Two sandwich?" she asked.

"One, thanks," I answered.

She rolled carpets of butter across two slices and went and retrieved a pot from her own table. She spread and chopped with a few professional flicks, and then handed me the meal on a plain white plate.

"Thanks very much, Edie," I said. I went back down the corridor. I held the plate high and kept my eyes fixed on the chunky irregular bread. I had never been given jam sandwiches for lunch before. I had never been left with such rough crusts.

Summer 1963

A few days after my eighteenth birthday, three weeks after I had left school, I was famous. I was more in the public eye than I would ever be again. I appeared on the front page of the *Sydney Morning Herald*, in the space reserved every year for what the paper called "top pupils". But I was a better than usual story. I was going to be a priest. I was giving up the frivolity, and the fame, of Sydney, and was going to Melbourne to become a Jesuit novice. "Top pupils" did Arts/Law or Medicine, but I was an example of idealism, of hedonism spurned. Or perhaps it was of senseless waste and the deep penetration of superstition. My family and school took the story as an endorsement of all they stood for. My grandmother had her doubts. She said the *Herald* was anti-Catholic and she "wondered", but the paper's tone gave nothing away.

I went to an end of school formal at the Australia Hotel. The bandleader called for silence; he had a message to read. He had been asked to announce an engagement between Gerard Windsor and Eve Shannon. I had never met the girl. There was a lot of clapping and catcalls and laughter, and a demand that we dance an engagement waltz together. I had heard of cruder jokes, and I suspected it was the doing of the wits of my year, Rodney Clark and James Loneragan, who both had brains and style, and it was not meant to be vindictive or cruel. So we danced the waltz together. When the dance was over Eve put an arum lily down her orange bodice, and I was not let go until I had plucked it out. She was blonde and aristocratically pretty and out of my class, and she married a merchant banker.

I was flown to Brisbane to farewell my grandfather. He took me to lunch at Lennons Hotel and made sure I was acting with my eyes open. By then he had been the doctor to every priest, brother and nun in Queensland for over forty years, and he knew more about priestly and religious matters than anyone in the country. I pared my chicken maryland elegantly while he probed, professionally, at motivation, other possibilities, postponement, influences. But if he saw any weakness he refused to exploit it. I could not have told whether he was against the venture. He remarked on the many fine men and great women he had known in the profession, and he added that it was of course as prone as any group of human beings to the excesses and lunacies that people were capable of. He let me glimpse trailers of the dramas he had seen — a nun constantly running about the streets of Brisbane and over the Story Bridge in her nightdress, a priest living in autocratic wilfulness as the legatee of the madam of a brothel. My imagination gasped, but my face was respectful and I concentrated on slivering the squash and the potato croquettes. My grandfather was an old Irishman, and I suspected he still had traces of the unreliability of his people.

I chose three books for the car trip to Melbourne. I had no interest in trying anything new, and just wanted the repetition of assured pleasures. In *The Savoy Operas* I checked myself on all the choruses and patter songs, and tried to make sure they were well stowed in the hold of my memory. Then I reread *The Magic Pudding*. I enjoyed it all, first, second, third, and fourth slices, and laughed a lot in the back of the car. My younger sister listened readily enough to the bits I read out and, without consulting the book, reeled off her own favourites, but largely she concentrated on her Virginia Woolf. My third book was *Beau Geste*, but its journey in pursuit of the grail was longer and more searing, its villains more successful, its triumph of good over evil far more limited, costly and ambiguous, and I didn't finish it before I got to Melbourne.

My family stayed overnight at the Windsor Hotel, and I had dinner there with them before they drove me out to Loyola College, the novitiate at Watsonia. Near the end of the meal I looked at my watch and said we had better be going. I said I would just go up to the room and get my port. My mother followed me up and came in the door just as I was lifting the bag. She threw her arms around me and broke into a sobbing cry. She held me tightly and cried that she would miss me terribly, that she had all the others, but that I was her eldest, I would always be her eldest. I was so embarrassed, so embarrassed. I had never felt my mother's breasts against me like that before. I held my hands lightly and tensely on her back. She stopped sobbing and said she wouldn't break down like that again.

There were twenty-three of us first year novices. We were called *animae*, souls, and in groups of two or three we were given into the care of a second year novice, an *angelus*, an angel. On the first Thursday in February, a day when the temperature reached the nineties, our *angeli* took us on a hike from Watsonia, through countless barbed wire fences and dunged and thistled paddocks, to a swimming hole on the Yarra called Lulu's. It must have been ten miles away, so we made a forced march of it. Being used to these hardships the *angeli* carried the packs, full of bread and jam and powdered cordial, and the *animae* carried the empty billies. My *angelus* had been at school with me, but my co-*animae* were older, strangers and men of the world. Michael Finnane had done two years Law, Ed Lourey had been a state public servant. Michael Finnane wiped his face constantly with a large handkerchief, and guffawed fruitily in between wipes, and complained that the Sydney University Regiment had never been like this. Ed Lourey chuckled and tossed out off-hand crackers of encouragement. I was full of awe for the virulence of their politics and the intemperateness of their language. They found our *angelus* simple, and winked and rolled their eyes, and complained that they hadn't sacrificed themselves to come down from Sydney to be put through this way of the cross just for the sake of a swim in the bloody Yarra. They were good-natured and kindly, and had a point.

At Lulu's we spread ourselves on the tumble of rocks and filled the billies with water from the river and sprinkled the cordial on the top. We changed modestly from our long trousers into togs, and tried the water, but not for long, most of us, because it was deep and fast-flowing and eddying there that summer. We went back to our jam sandwiches, and filling-in of backgrounds and testing the figurative water really for the years ahead together. We kept our shirts on because the General of the Jesuits had issued a letter not long before forbidding sunbaking, and in that busy, talk-hungry, laughing circle of souls and angels we began to get a feel for a set of ethics and values more refined and yet more tangible than anything we could have dreamed of.

And about half past two an *angelus*, not mine, realised he had not seen one of his *animae* for at least an hour. Several of the *angeli*, sportsmen and stronger swimmers, dived, but the river was muddy as well as turbulent. The main party of us, all the *animae*, left before the police divers came and found him in a hole, thirty feet down.

Michael Liston, we were told, automatically became a vowed Jesuit at the moment of death. He was coffined wearing a clerical collar and the Jesuit soutane. We had not expected to go out into civilisation for many months after we entered, but we were all taken in buses to bury our contemporary and colleague in the Jesuit plot in Kew cemetery among the bones of numerous old men who had gone far into their dotage in the service of God. Later we were told, and adopted, the axiom that Jesuit funerals were cheerful, family affairs. But I still see Michael Liston's mother, young and slim, behind a black mantilla, standing above his coffin. I told myself, as I watched, that she was unrecriminating, that she had been willing to give up her son, that he had only wanted God's service, and that God knew what served Him best.

Raising the Mind and Heart

Catholic Catechism on "Prayer"

When I was a child and staying with my grandmother in Murrurundi she slept me in the front room that had been her own parents' bedroom. Only the hedge and the orange tree shielded it from the main street, the road that linked the New England Tableland with the Liverpool Plains. In the front room I lay in the centre of things. Down Main Street was the bakery and its sweet smell reached back to my grandmother's general store. The store was on the other side of the wall across the corridor from my bedroom. Past where I lay was the bank and Dr Middleton's and then the Pages River. Once you went across the river there was the post office and the library and the oval. It was from the front room you most distinctly heard the old bridge twitching and creaking. The sound only stopped for the quickfire exercise of wooden scales when wheels spun across the polished planks.

On the mantelpiece on the far wall of the room was a votive lamp. When I came to bed the wick was already alight. It rode on its tin disc, bobbing steady in its saucer of oil. The Sacred Heart stood behind it, his arms stretched out low in front of his body. There were other objects and shapes along the mantelpiece, but the lamp was for him, and for me. I lay with the lamp on my left and the window on my right and faced out across the corridor to the closed door of the sitting room where the adults were talking. Before I closed my eyes the small tip of flame, in the sharp collar of its float, was bending and rearing and flickering and holding steady. The vitality never waned. As I went and came and went again across the boundaries of sleep, the shadow of Christ was the only thing I could see. He was immense, he loomed, he moved up the wall. He trembled, pinned up there against the flat blankness. But he broke away and slid easily from side to side. Then he moved down, gathering himself in till he was someone I knew and his hands were moving together to pat mine or to lift me up. Over my eyes his shadow rose and fell. I breathed in easily to the exhilaration of him, and breathed out just as steadily to the red glow that sustained him. The hum or murmur or sudden variation of the adults' talk, the hurl or rainy hiss of vehicles, the dash of headlights, the steady arcs of streetlights, all passed across the screen of my eyelids and were absorbed into the one ceaseless drama on the walls around me.

For the eight years I was at school at Riverview my place in the chapel was marked by my *Alter Christus*, my school prayer book. The blue endpapers had a photo of the school and the opening verse of the "*Lauda Sion Salvatorem*" and lines for my name and address and the printed instruction "I am a Catholic. In case of accident or serious illness, please call a priest and notify ..." I filled in my father's name and then my mother's name. The *Alter Christus* would somehow be accompanying me wherever I went.

It contained more than prayers. It had information about Days of Fast and Abstinence and the customary seasons for Nuptial Masses and practical suggestions for acts of self-denial and quotations from Popes and men and women of God. While waiting for the chapel to fill or Mass to start or after Communion I liked to browse in the *Alter Christus*. Again and again I returned to the swingeing cry of Cardinal Newman: "Alas, alas, for those who die without fulfilling their mission; who were called to be holy and who lived in sin; who were called to worship Christ and who plunged into this giddy and unbelieving world; who were called to fight and who remained idle. Alas for those who have had gifts and talents and who have not used, or misused, or abused them! The world goes on from age to age, but the holy

Angels and blessed Saints are always crying alas, alas, and woe, woe, over the loss of vocations, and the disappointments of hopes, and the scorn of God's love, and the ruin of souls."

I had read nothing else by Newman, but the chorus of his phrases, the authority of his pronouncement, was a trumpet across my soul every time I stopped at his page in the *Alter Christus*. That he was not a saint somehow gave him more weight. Just as it did to the words of Père Lacordaire four pages earlier: "To live in the midst of the world without wishing its pleasures, to be a member of each family, yet belonging to none; to share all sufferings; to penetrate all secrets; to heal all wounds; to go from men to God and offer him their prayers; to return from God to man to bring pardon and hope; to have a heart of fire by charity and a heart of bronze by chastity; to teach, console, and bless always; my God, what a life! And it is yours, O priest of Jesus Christ!"

In my last year at school, when I was head prefect and had my own prie-dieu at the back of the chapel, I could look at the data I had entered in the back of the *Alter Christus*. My baptism, First Communion, Confirmation, entrance to Riverview, and my reception into all the school sodalities.

After that there were no markers given for my spiritual progress. I slid the neat, navy, gilt-embossed book left to right and back again along the shelf of my prie-dieu.

The Third Division Debating Society met in the evening of the last Friday of the month. All Third Division boarders belonged to it. Anyone could be called upon to speak. There were elected office-bearers and the meetings were formal, but the Division Prefect held discreet control. We crowded into the Third Division Library down in the basement, and the mild oppression of rotting fruit and unwashed sports clothes drifted across us from the haggard tin lockers. We jostled elbow to elbow and were allowed to sit hunched in the wide sandstone embrasures of the windows. The Division Prefect, Mr O'Sullivan, stood just inside the door and stilled the babble by rolling slightly on the balls of his feet and clenching his hands under his chin. He said the "Hail Mary" and then moved to the back corner of the room and sat down, wrapping his gown around his knees and tying its wings across his chest. He had organised the night's agenda, and with his index finger playing away at his clerical collar, he nodded to the office-bearers and the meeting began.

After the Minutes were read there was a two-man debate. Michael Cannon affirmed that Country was better than City; the air was healthy, Australia rode on the sheep's back, you learnt things like driving much sooner, you were a real help to your old man. Freddie Cahill spoke for the City: there was much more to do, beaches and pictures and things, you needed the city to run things, Sydney Harbour and the bridge was the best-known thing about Australia. A vote was taken. The House divided along party lines. The verdict was for Country.

Richard Chisholm stood up. He gave an itchy grin of antici-pation and recited several pages of something made up of Spoonerisms. He didn't trip up once, and the faltering, delayed laughter of the members of the Debating Society encouraged him to signal his punchlines boldly. His feat was recognised and cheers and whistles swamped the clapping when he finished.

I was next and last. I was thirteen and I had to recite Cam-pion's "Brag". Mr O'Sullivan had lent me Evelyn Waugh's *Edmund Campion*, and the complete "Brag" was reproduced as an appendix. Mr O'Sullivan had suggested I leave out some of the detailed argument in the middle and concentrate on the beginning and end. I stepped up on to the teacher's platform. I explained to the members of the Debating Society that Edmund Campion wrote his Brag in 1580 to Queen Elizabeth's Privy Councillors setting forth the purpose of his vocation and his mission in England. I saw in dozens of eyes a sliding retreat from any further prospect of fun. "Right Honourable," I addressed my fellows, and I saw smiles and cocked questioning faces. I lifted my gaze to the back wall among the honour boards, and

I put my hands together behind my back and I delivered the testament. I let the words ring. "Many innocent hands are lifted up to heaven for you daily by those English students, whose posteritie shall never die, which beyond seas, gathering virtue and sufficient knowledge for the purpose, are determined never to give you over, but either to win you heaven, or to die upon your pikes. And touching our Societie, be it known to you that we have made a league — all the Jesuits in the world, whose succession and multitude must overreach all the practices of England — cheerfully to carry the cross you shall lay upon us, and never to despair your recovery, while we have a man left to enjoy your Tyburn, or to be racked with your torments, or consumed with your prisons. The expense is reckoned, the enterprise is begun; it is of God, it cannot be withstood. So the faith was planted: so it must be restored."

I wanted to be applauded, but I sensed it was not quite a moment for the Third Division Debating Society's type of applause. The other members must have agreed and gave the looking-around, uncurling clap that winds up a meeting. Mr O'Sullivan said to me quietly that I had done the "Brag" very well.

Watsonia was a word I first understood when I was seven. I was still in my unselfconscious, single-digit years when I wrote a school essay about what I was going to be when I grew up, and I wrote that I was going to Watsonia. Not that the resolution survived so openly or healthily into adolescence. But it haunted me. The priesthood was incomparably the single most worthwhile thing to do with one's life, and God's finger beckoned in a hard-headed, no-nonsense way. His signs were easily read. Yes, I was in good health, I was leading a good life, I was competent at my studies. I didn't want messages, but I knew these facts were flashes from God's fingernail. I was good at Classics, I was a reasonable public speaker, and Law, the obvious worldly opening for me, I could feel no quiver of interest in. My ticket was marked for the Society of Jesus. Still I would not pick it up. I was sixteen when I did my Leaving Certificate, but I returned to school because I did not yet know, I said, what I wanted to do when I left.

In August, at a dance with Loreto Kirribilli at the Cammeray Bowling Club I fell in love during the Pride of Erin. It was the night before I went to Singleton to cadet camp. The girl was a boarder in term time and lived interstate during the holidays, and so all we could do was correspond. We wrote openly to one another at school. I rode high into my last term, my spirits sharp and euphoric, not reeling and dulled as I thought they might have been had the affair been more proximate and more bodily. She wrote to me as I wrote to her — without declarations, without plans. She let me know, delicately, that she had heard, though not from me, of the possibilities for my life. She neither protested nor encouraged, just dealt the possibility face up between us in its stark but glowing offer. Then one letter — I have no idea why — dislodged me. Perhaps released me. Father Carroll had slipped it under the door of my room, as usual, and it was there when I arrived back from the oval just after five o'clock. I had been coaching junior sprinters. I read the generous looping words and I knew then that I would have to go, and I would go. I went into the shower room. There was no one there at this hour, between seasons, and I washed alone. I dressed and then I went to the chapel, in through the nearest side door. I blessed myself beside the RAAF Memorial. The old boys killed in the air supported the brightest window in the building. Robert Bellarmine, Doctor of the Church, talked with the young saints of the Society of Jesus, still splendid in all their secular colour. I moved into the far corner and I knelt and the prayer gushed out of me. It was gratitude and resolution and the joy of release and the intense happiness of duty accepted. I stayed in the chapel running trills up and down my soul until the bell sounded for tea.

The nub of it all thereafter was to keep going. Elijah, weary, hungry and thirsty, found a little cake and a flask of water, and he ate and drank, and on the strength of that food he walked forty days and forty nights until he came to the mountain of God.

Five weeks after I went to Watsonia I performed the Spiritual Exercises of Saint Ignatius. We referred to it simply as "doing the Long Retreat." Thirty days of concentrated prayer and silence. If I could endure this, I might endure the longer haul. I could gain from it the vision and the sustenance for my lifetime's march. For four hours every day I listened to the Master of Novices. For another five I prayed, rubbing the fuel and the balm of the Gospel into my soul. God made the world in love. He would end it in the same way. And at this moment in the history of salvation Christ called me, and I pledged my service. For a month I saw and heard nothing but this plan. My mind and my imagination were tethered, gladly, in its lushness. For thirty days I was in a high remote place with him, and he was transfigured before me. When I came back in from this, my own peculiar desert, I hugged my vision to keep it with me.

So, as a novice, my normal state was silence. There were times for talk — after meals, at games or outdoor work — but the norm was silence. The fragile well of prayer in us was not to be smothered by the accretive silt of talk and distraction. Our souls were best left to themselves, undisturbed. We only spoke about necessary matters, and then in Latin. After night prayers silence covered us entirely. This was Major Silence or *Magnum Silentium*. In these hours our company was strictly Christ. This was the night, "when no man works", when Nicodemus came secretly to Jesus, and also when "the devil goes about like a ravening lion seeking whom he may devour". Our sole refuge was with God. In the still of the house Major Silence was a type of the awesome stillness of the universe rocking in the cradle of God's hand. When the seventh seal was opened, the Book of the

Apocalypse told us, there was silence in heaven for about half an hour. We stilled our own lives, tasted the peace of heaven.

It was not the night that could send the spectre of depression to squat on my eighteen-year-old soul. I was too tired, I slept too soundly. It was the call, the 5.25 a.m. call, that could wind me. As I woke my limbs felt all the heaviness of the long day and the long life of such discipline that lay ahead. Every day of my life rising to a bell at 5.25 a.m. There was a phrase that carried all the burden of that future. When I inspected the noticeboard after breakfast, it bore most frequently the words "*De More*", "according to custom" or "the usual". There was to be no break from routine. On a Melbourne winter's day the prospect of *De More* was one that I could only allow myself to note, and then move purposefully, to the next specific half-hour task. There was no dwelling on *De More*.

I clasped at the vision. The Lord had called in the night to the boy Samuel. He called me just as certainly every morning at 5.25. In the winter I was warned by the heater pipes coughing and groaning their way into life. In summer, when the dormitory windows were open, I heard the crunching, arthritic steps of Brother Stamp hastening across the gravel to the bell tower. He pulled on the rope and rang out twelve loud low strokes. At the very first I jumped from the bed. The Rule told me to do so. To move at the first sound as if at the voice of an angel. Other unseen beds creaked and slippers slid and clapped across the wooden floor. I reached for my dressing gown and, with the other seven in each dormitory, I caught my breath and broke into a loud feverish "*Te Deum*", spitting out the opening fricatives, a gabble of defiance against the dark forces circling my spirit. My eyes were closed and I yanked the cord around my waist and cried out "*Te Deum Laudamus, Te Dominum Confitemur, Te Aeternum Patrem Omnis Terra Veneratur*" I seized my toilet bag and thrummed away at the universal praise. We stood, each of us, just inside the closed curtains of our cubicles and tumbled out our faith and hope. "*In Te Domine Speravi. Non Confundar in*

Aeternum." "I shall not ever be confounded". We flung the curtains back. The rings clashed wildly, we scrambled for the door and raced for the showers. The Latin had gashed my brain and the old ode went on and on, throbbing in my morning skull. My head was a tangle of warm water and awkward pig Latin and Sunlight soap and the assault on heaven.

Six months after I entered the novitiate the Master of Novices withdrew the "*Te Deum*". We were to substitute the ninety-ninth Psalm. It was short, and it was to be in English. "Acclaim the Lord, all the earth," we answered the bell. "Serve the Lord with gladness. Go into his presence with great joy."

On the Society's Terms

It was when I went to the Jesuits to school in 1950 that I first heard another language. The expression, when you wished to be excused from the class, was "Square, please sir?" You went to the square, there was no talking in the square, the square was out of bounds unless you were there for the one practical reason. The usage was never queried. When you were at home you reverted quite unselfconsciously from square to toilet or lavatory or bathroom or whatever the familial term was. The word square was part of what made a school of the Irish Jesuit tradition unique. The term's origins are not recorded. Its use was entrenched at Clongowes Wood College in County Kildare in the 1880s. Certain fellows were caught smugging "in the square one night", Stephen Dedalus tells us.

The Jesuit education of my four brothers and myself overlapped without a break. I began in 1950, the youngest finished in 1977. When I left Riverview in 1962, square was the only term I had ever heard or used. Yet my brother Guy, for example, who began there in 1968, never encountered the word at all.

Square was specifically a school term. It was not used in seminaries or university colleges or houses where Jesuits trained their own young men. Theirs was another language again.

On each novice's desk was a cyclostyled booklet. It was entitled *COPIA VERBORUM*, A Supply of Words. Most hours of our day any talk was in Latin, and when we needed a word we went to the *Copia Verborum* and found one. The words were concrete and utilitarian, not the vocabulary of Cicero or Virgil. The *Copia Verborum* gave us broom, duster, toilet, shower, jam, coffee, verandah, collar, soccer ball. The book's covers and pages were pierced and held together by two brass studs. The possibility existed of opening the pins and inserting other pages, but that was never found necessary.

Latin was our language's source, even when it was not its medium. This Latin was colloquial and used with the utmost casualness. It was shorthand yet it invoked a complete metaphysic. We came, for example, from IN MUNDO as in "When I was *in mundo*." Literally the phrase translated as "in the world". It referred to where we came from before we entered religious life. It was where our parents and siblings still were. Of course the derivation lay in such phrases as "the world, the flesh and the devil", the traditional enemies of the human soul and particularly of those deliberately seeking after sanctity. So the world was a noxious place, an inherently evil concept, and for centuries "world" had been the word used for a summary description of the convert's rejectamenta: "He turned his back on the world and entered a monastery;" or, "The world with all its glamour and false promises no longer held any attraction for him, so he retired to a desert place."

I accepted this fundamental dichotomy. It was useful to be able to speak of and partially disown the commonplace or disedifying elements of our past lives by noting them as taking place *in mundo*. But I sensed, distantly, the self-righteousness in this. After all, my family, my old friends were still *in mundo* and would be remaining there. It was the Latin that allowed us to be easy in the use of the term. Oddly the foreignness domesticated the evil. There was even a soft affection, not a nostalgia, when we spoke of that alien universe where so many of our ties and memories still belonged.

When there was no value judgment involved it was easy to slip back into English, albeit a simple translation from the Latin.

So while there was the evaluative distinction between those who lived *in mundo* and those who had consecrated themselves to God, there was also the further, merely descriptive, distinction between Jesuits and everyone else. There were OURS and there were EXTERNS. "Ours" was commonly used in the context of a limitation upon the readership of books and documents. "For the Use of Ours Only," they were headed. *Ad Usum Nostrorum Tantum.* It had the advantage of being, or appearing to be, less self-centred, especially when in the presence of Externs. "Many of Ours there?" — at the match, at the funeral, at the Gilbert & Sullivan, we could ask discreetly, and any self-absorption would not be immediately apparent.

Yet Ours could also be derogatory. It had one strikingly facetious use. It appeared in the acronym TARBO, a Typical Affair Run By Ours. In short, a cock-up for which Jesuits were primarily and ultimately responsible. There were limits however to the legitimate uses of the term. A tarbo referred to such matters as transport arrangements, liturgical events, the hosting of cricket matches or afternoon teas — enterprises that were never considered areas of Jesuit professional expertise. A tarbo could never refer to, say, the way a school was run, or a retreat given.

The occurrence of even the worst tarbos was not brought to the attention of Externs. Externs were all other humankind, the objects of the apostolic endeavours of the Society of Jesus, but seen in this instance, according to a careful priority, as outsiders, as people who had no business being involved in our Jesuit family life. The Pope for example was an extern. Externs might well be in our midst. Leo Daly, the kitchenhand who was intellectually slow, and whose hair was a Boofhead crest with a splash of white at the front of the comb, was an Extern. He had a flat in a small cottage to the rear of the garages. He was the one Extern always in our presence, and he was simple.

Leo's flat was actually inside CLAUSURA. *Clausura* translated as cloister, but we never translated it. It was the area into which no female was allowed. Our front door opened on to a marble-paved hallway, with a parlour on each side. But the door at the far end of the hallway was marked *clausura*. We used the word readily. *Clausura* was one of the key elements that defined our life. The term was so alien that it could be tamed easily and made our own. Cloister, on the other hand, was an unassimilable word. Monks had cloister, a cloister was the covered ambulatory of an enclosed courtyard. But we were not monks, we were a modern order, we were open to the world. We were not cloistered men. We had *clausura*.

The term MONKS, however, was used. It occurred in the phrase "the Watsie monks", as in "Regards to all the Watsie monks" and "I must come out and say hello to the Watsie monks". It was used, that is, by other, older Jesuits in training, men who had gone on to a further stage in another house. Largely, to us, this meant the university students at Campion College in Kew, and the equivalent phrase we used when we were referring to them was "the Campion schols". "Monks" designated the scholastics at Watsonia (though it did not include the novices). The term suggested the sequestered, self-contained life lived in that outer suburb as opposed to the sophisticated freedom of undergraduates resident in one of Melbourne's well-heeled inner suburbs. We at Watsonia didn't use the word monks of ourselves, and it may even have been passing out of use.

We were SCHOLASTICS. Even as novices we were *novitii scholastici*. It was not actually a religious designation. We were defined by our major public activity; we were in school. We were primarily in school, as it happened, to scholastic philosophy and theology. Other seminarians or religious for whom this was also the prescribed course were not known as scholastics. They were students, a term so general as to be without content, whereas, as scholastics, we were given up to study, to learning, to a tradition, and to the leisure needed to maximise them all.

We were new in religion and were still shaking out our identity. We were learning the particularity of the Jesuit vocation. We were not monks, a creation of the sixth century. We were Jesuits, appreciative of the genius of the past, but not ourselves shackled by it. Yet we found ourselves using a term cognate with "monks". Amongst the locals, the Externs that is, of the suburb of Watsonia, the institution we lived in was known as the monastery. This was understandable. Our neighbours were using the simple, familiar term. If we had to identify ourselves or give directions we referred to the monastery.

The property was a presence in the suburb. Because it was so big, because the building was, from some locations, glimpsed but never wholly seen, because of the perennial oddity of religious life, and because of the high-towered bell that rang every day, first to wake us and then at the hours of the Angelus, and that could not be stopped penetrating beyond our borders, the monastery became a definer of the locality. It was a grey building, a three-storeyed E rendered in pebbled stucco and cement. It was angular without being proportioned, and was crowned by a squat, battlemented tower. Around it stretched a domain of rough lawns and paths and an oval and a sloping paddock and tennis and basketball courts and shrines and a hen run and a vegetable garden and garages and Externs' cottages and a stand of almond trees and a clutch of beehives.

We controlled rather than cultivated our property. As novices we worked it for at least three hours each day, and most of what we did was cleaning and scouring. Inside and out. Each work group was led by a DUX. In the scullery, for example, he led a team of four, allotted to *prima machina, secunda machina, argentum*, and *in vasario*, loading and unloading the dishwasher, drying the silver, and scrubbing the pots and pans in the sink. We raced through the steam and sweat of the scullery, bouncing the plates into racks, levering up the steel drop-gate of the dishwasher, clashing the rack in, tossing the spoonfuls of soap, triggering the stormburst of hot water. We lowered our heads into the stale, rolling mists of steam and ran up along our arm a stack of cleaned and fiery plates. In the afternoons two of us stood outside the scullery window and hoisted the grate from the grease traps. The smell was strong and vile, but I took a pleasure in skimming the white fatty crust from the surface of the drain, and then returning again and again to pick off the ever smaller globules still floating in the unbound water.

The grease traps were on the Bungay Street side of the property, the part of the building nearest to other dwellings. The traps had a run-off outlet for their excess water. It surfaced about fifty yards from the scullery, nearer again to the boundary, and then ran nowhere for about another fifty yards down a narrow finger-deep furrow. We called this the CLOACA MAXIMA. Literally the phrase translated as "the great sewer", but it was not that. It was simply our *cloaca max*. A faint steam hung over it most of the time, and a furry grey slime tended to form along the sides and bottom, and then slip free and coagulate so that eventually the clots became a dam against the passage of the water. Twice a week a pair of novices were assigned to walk the length of the *cloaca max* and flick out these emboli with short-handled spades and scrape or slice the sides of the channel.

Inside the house we had the VIA MAX. It was the long corridor that went the length of the front of the building. Novices waxed and polished and mopped the *via max*. Going to meals or chapel or the front door we had to pass through the *via max*. Twelve feet across, it was unbroken by furniture or protuberances of any kind. The long cast of the eye was undistracted. When we walked along it together, in answer to the bell in the morning for Mass or in the evening for night prayers, we always kept to the wall nearest the quadrangle. Priests and brothers might come down the middle, and the Rector, Father O'Donovan, even swung along the far side, pumping his closed fist against the wall towards the front of the house. But novices came from the

south, scholastics from the north, and we descended the stairs
at either end of the *via max* and, in two files, at a brisk but
reverent pace, beside but not touching the wall, we converged
on the chapel door. The length and the unencumbered line of
the *via max* tugged me, as it might have tugged any walker,
towards action and speed and the vigorous exploitation of its
space, but I resisted. I did not look up and ahead. I kept my eyes
on the back of the man in front and hugged the wall.

As a novice I was in the care of the *Magister Novitiorum*,
Master of Novices. If we spoke of FATHER MASTER, the context
had some solemnity. We were summoning up or responding to
an aura of authority. Whereas if he were being invoked as more
or less just another individual in our community, we referred to
him as the MAG NOV. Again the Latin was more comradely and
informal. But he was always referred to by his office and with
the definite article. The person actually holding the office was
Father John Monahan, but we never used such a personal designation. Our parents might refer to Father Monahan and write
to Father Monahan, but if the surname was ever heard amongst
ourselves it was without the title and it was a sign of truculence
and bad blood, and I wondered. Jesuits a little older than ourselves would refer to him as Sean Monahan, but the import of
this usage was shifty; it sounded like a claim to some comrade-
ship, a boast that the hierarchical gap had been bridged, and a
recommendation to us that we were in the hands of a good man.
It seemed a pointed underlining of his Irishness, though in fact
I had no reason to doubt that he had been christened John. The
use of Sean seemed to signify both fellowship and a just slightly
contemptible alienness. I never heard him addressed as Sean,
and when we had passed beyond his supervision we still called
him Father, but referred to him by the affectionate diminutive,
Mon.

The Master of Novices had an assistant, called his SOCIUS.
This term was never translated; we referred always, quite

simply, to the *Socius*. The Latin word had a volume of meanings, none of which could be suitably translated for our context. In Latin primers a *socius* was an ally; *socius* was a politico-military term. In a Jesuit historical context we were aware that we were of the Society of Jesus, that is, we ourselves were *socii Jesu*. The earliest group of Jesuits were referred to as Ignatius and his companions. They were his *socii*. But our *Socius* was not, and was not intended to be, a companion for our master of novices, and certainly not for ourselves. The *Socius* attended to our physical or at least secular welfare; he would be the one to admonish us over public breaches of discipline or religious decorum. He had a word to novices whose heads bounced and swivelled and never observed custody of the eyes. He noticed dirty gowns or shoes. He took to task novices who idled and talked too much when they were working in the garden at what we called outdoor manuals. He asked novices to step on to the scales and pointed out to them that they were overweight. Masters of Novices stayed in office for many years, as many as twenty, but the position of *Socius* saw a ready turnover; the position seemed, even to a novice, to have something about it too secondary and provisional; it was marking time. The *Socius* represented not the spiritual life, but the commissariat and base needed to support that life. In this case such a distinction was heightened because the *Socius* was a Sydney man, an old boy of the Christian Brothers at Waverley, and a fine swimmer, whereas the Master of Novices was a Dubliner, a Jesuit old boy, and a one-lunged victim of tuberculosis. I had come to religion for a life beyond anything I had known and it was there in the Master of Novices rather than in the *Socius*. Yet I made no distinction between the piety of each man.

As well as the priests there were the "brothers". For two years, while we were novices, we used the title "Brother" to and of one another. We were not to use Christian names. This title followed by the surname was all that was licit. When we took vows we could use Christian names, and we advanced to the title "Mister". But only those whose goal was the priesthood. There were also those fellow novices who would go on being brothers after they had taken vows. Traditionally they had been called "lay brothers", but the term was not accurate. These men were religious, not lay people, and by the 1960s they were being called COADJUTOR BROTHERS or, more correctly, temporal coadjutors. Their role was that of a secular support system for the spiritual ministrations of the priests. They were (and generally came from) the working class. In 1963 they still carried marks of distinction, even discrimination. They wore narrow, cut-down clerical collars, they took recreation together and not with the priests, they sat at the bottom of the refectory, and their gowns lacked the flaps of cloth, known as wings, that hung backwards from the shoulders.

There had been vowed brothers at Riverview, but they had rarely been involved directly with the boys. The exception was Brother Johnson who kept and distributed the boarders' pocket money, entering hieroglyphic strokes of red ink in his leather ledgers. He had a limp so pronounced that he was on a constant lean to port. The boys referred to him as Pegleg Scrooge. Other Brothers were further removed. The school was pitted with plaques recording that this building or that hot water system had been "donated by a friend of Brother Doyle". Brother Doyle, long before my time, had been his own best friend, and the additions to the school had been a way of laundering his speculations in the stock market. No pupil had ever known that. The more regular example of a brother was Michael O'Brien. He ran a herd of milkers whose cowpats we used to hurl at one another during slow times in the cricket outfield. As a ten year old I passed Brother O'Brien ambling back into the school buildings, always in the company of a fox terrier named Spot. He would smile and make some kind of Irish noise from under his old fedora. He died in the evening of the feast of Saint Ignatius 1957, and when the Rector announced this to the boarders we knelt and said a decade of the Rosary for him between the first and second reels of *The Student Prince*.

When I went to Watsonia I was living with such men. Or at least with brothers. It was a social immersion rare for someone of my background. I would not have experienced it had I gone to university. Senior vowed brothers, the ones at Watsonia, were fabled to be shrewd men, to have an unerring eye for a good novice or for the one who would not persevere. It was an atmospheric belief that, being occupied with temporal matters, they had their feet on the ground. In our own work in the refectory or the scullery or the grounds we rubbed up against the brothers in a way we never did with the priests. Leaning on the pantry shelves, replacing butters in the freezer room, we found the brothers, even as they were assessing us, almost intimate, even conspiratorial the way they talked about the priests in the house, especially those they might refer to as "the senior Fathers". We always observed the formality of address-ing them as "Brother", but some novices would refer to them with a familiarity never allowed for priests. They were adopted as family more readily. Maurie Joyce, Jack O'Callaghan, Leo Cussen, Vic Manning, Jack Stamp. The diminutives and shorten-ers, the no-nonsense names of Australian men.

One brother's name was odd. Lemuel Timanus. Lem was not really a brother. He was an Extern, but he actually lived with us. He had a permanent room in the retreat house, the long wing that constituted the back of the E that was the building. Lem called himself an auxiliary brother. As far as I knew Lem was the only Jesuit "auxiliary brother" in the world. It suited both parties that he should live among us and work for us and be given this nominal fellowship with us. Technically he was an Extern and followed his own routine and rule. He liked a conversation, and even Major Silence meant nothing to him. He was very elderly and tall, with the facial skin of a baby's bottom.

He walked with a rolling limp and spoke at a very high pitch. "Brother," he would call from the dark of the corridor, and his index finger would bob. It was hard to ignore an importunate cripple. To be engaged by him in conversation was "to be caught by Lem". But he spent a long day outside at work. He was in charge of the vegetable patch, and he decided on its uses and acquired and nursed the seeds and seedlings and did all the planting. He approached scholastics to do the unskilled labour for him. Once I was a scholastic and studying philosophy I wanted exercise that was simple and vigorous. To work for Lem was also useful, and no partner was required. Lem's favoured produce was broad beans. He could never have enough long, heaped beds. So I dug them for him, acre after acre. I was determined to get my exercise in economical time. I did not idle with Lem. I knew, and asked, nothing of his past. His present seemed transparent. But he reminded me, he reminded everyone, over and over that he was an auxiliary brother.

"I know, Lem," I told him. "You're unique."

Lem edged closer and clasped the straps of his overalls. I pressed my foot down on the shaft of my spade.

"That's not all, Brother." There was a milkiness about Lem. His white hair and his regular, mobile teeth and this unbroken voice rising from the convex softness of him.

"Why isn't it all, Lem?"

"I've spoken to a senior Father of the Society. He says that before I die, Brother, before I die, I'll be allowed to take my vows in the Society. As a coadjutor brother."

"That's wonderful, Lem." I stepped back off my spade.

"He says I will have been here long enough by then for it to be counted as a noviceship."

"I should think so, Lem." I had never heard of any date of Lem's arrival at Watsonia, or of anyone who had been there before he came. I was a transient. All my fellow novices, fellow scholastics, were transients. Lem alone was a permanent resident of Watsonia. I leant on the spade and again I sliced hard into the organic mix of Lem's plot.

Our Conversation Is in Heaven

Philippians 3.20

In free time I learnt 250 lines of the *Aeneid*. Free time came in small segments. The first of the day was at 12.30 p.m., for just a quarter of an hour. The last was at 8 p.m. and extended for a luxurious half hour. Otherwise free time was in five minute allotments. In free time we could read. Whatever we liked. From our library, a library of spiritual theology, biblical studies, sermons, devotional works, ecclesiastical and Jesuit history, and nothing secular. Or we could read from among our textbooks. Along the Rosary Path or looking out over the verandah towards the chapel I read and reread and learnt by heart Virgil's account of Aeneas's visit to Hades; all the swirling life of the underworld and his great panorama of the dead.

> *huc omnis turba ad ripas effusa ruebat.*
> *matres atque viri defunctaque corpora vita*
> *magnanimum heroum, pueri innuptaeque puellae,*
> *impositique rogis iuvenes ante ora parentum:*
> *quam multa in silvis autumni frigore primo*
> *lapsa cadunt folia, aut ad terram gurgite ab alto*
> *quam multae glomerantur aves, ubi frigidus annus*
> *trans pontum fugat et terris immittit apricis.*
> *stabant orantes primi transmittere cursum*
> *tendebantque manus ripae ulterioris amore.*
> *navita sed tristis nunc hos nunc accipit illos,*
> *ast alios longe summotos arcet harena.*

As novices we were to immerse ourselves in the spiritual

world, and so we were cut off from the secular one. We had no access to radio or television or magazines or newspapers. Bare exceptions to this rule had been introduced by our novice master in the year before I arrived; at morning tea he laid out on a table a selection of small cuttings he had made from the previous day's *Age*. On late Saturday afternoons he pinned up the VFL scores. I could take or leave the matters chosen for my interest.

On 23 November 1963 we were at lunch in the refectory. Lunch was always taken in silence while some secular book was read aloud to us from the pulpit there for perhaps ten minutes. The religious readings and the notices were confined to dinner. But at lunch on 23 November 1963 the reader began not with the title of the book but with the Society's motto *Ad Majorem Dei Gloriam*, the invariable prefix to an official notice. "Your charitable prayers," began the reader in a formal, even voice — and we wondered which older Jesuit had died — "are requested for the repose of the soul of President Kennedy who was killed today." The reader put the white card down on the ledge of the pulpit and took up the book. I tucked my serviette into my gown and poured water for those near me and, waiting for the servers to distribute the plates, bent my face to the thick varnished wood of the table.

We were prohibited certain topics of conversation. They were listed in the noviceship Customs Book, a black, steel-ring folder, and were called simply Forbidden Topics.

1. *Schools and School Life*. We were to be universal men; there was no place for cliques or provincialism or the backward look.

2. *Eating and Drinking*. Food and drink were necessary, but for the mind to rest on them or the tongue to dwell on them was to give in to the carnality of our natures. No real distinction was to be made between epicures and alcoholics and other prisoners of the needs of our flesh. So novices did not

stimulate one another with visions of cuisine or memories of binges. Even if we referred, illicitly, to the food actually set before us, it was never with the passions of either salivation or distaste. We groaned at Brother O'Callaghan's green jelly, but it was not the texture or the taste of the food we were rejecting. It was the genial unimaginativeness of the slow-working brother whom we all liked and who had no talent for cooking. Novices ate with gusto, and that was not a matter for censure. One day of Church fast, Father Gryst, the priest responsible for the material welfare of the house, strode the length of the refectory, in the middle of lunch, and gave a sharp instruction to the cook that something more was to be prepared at once for the novices' meal. Few of them were twenty-one, he pointed out, and they were not obliged to fast. We ate what we wanted and we enjoyed it, but we were not to go further. When Father Kurts, the *Socius*, polished us for a someday appearance at "the governor's board", as he put it, it was to ensure that our observance of etiquette and decorum never detracted from our impact as religious men. The board itself, in my imagination, was bare.

3. "... *or other subjects unbecoming religious conversation.*" The embargo on food and drink contained a further phrase. No more needed to be said, and even that much was labouring the point. "For our conversation is in heaven," wrote St Paul, and "in heaven there is neither marrying nor giving in marriage".

4. *Anything learnt by breach of the rules.* We were not to compound the first failing. We were bound to silence and to custody of the eyes. We were forbidden to read waste paper, of any kind, and we were forbidden to speak with Externs. At work in the kitchen or the scullery we were often in the presence of Externs, Leo Daly or Jack Outlaw who were kitchenhands. They were bound by no rules restricting their

conversation. In their flats they had radios and televisions. They were interested in worldly matters, racing results and so forth, and they didn't hesitate to talk about them. It was a difficult situation for novices. Stan Hogan exchanged opinions with Jack Outlaw on fast tracks at Flemington or Randwick, and on the relative merits of Roy Higgins or K. Langby being up. But he observed a distance by addressing as "Mr Outlaw" a man otherwise universally known as Jack. There was always pressure on our dyke against the world, and I wondered at the stratagems to hold or circumvent it. We were not to pass on anything Externs had told us. Other than at recreation or "on villa" or in class or in dealing with superiors, our rules for speech were simple: we were to talk only *de rebus necessariis*, on necessary matters, and then it was to be in Latin. A New South Welshman, I could barely put together all the languages when I heard Michael McKernan say in September, the month of the Brownlow Medal, that he had been passing through the scullery and he had heard a voice — he didn't identify it — crying aloud *"Skilton vicit"*.

5. *Penances*. They were not to be aired in recreation or jokingly or in the context of an individual. Yet Penances remained our keenest temptation. They were particular to our life. They were such an intimate family taboo. The history, the morals, the mechanics of Penances teased us for attention. We read about them all the time. Only in a formal, impersonal context were we allowed to speak of them. There were three traditional instruments of physical penance: the hairshirt, the chain and the discipline. We did not use hairshirts, rough prickly animal coats worn next to the skin. Presumably hairshirts were complicated in manufacture and fitting. But we each had our own chain and discipline, and they were manufactured by the novice holding the office of Tradesman. Novitiate offices lasted six weeks, but the skill

involved and acquired in his office usually ensured that a novice was Tradesman for three months. He shared a work-room with the seamster directly under the central tower, and for forty minutes each morning from Monday to Friday he manufactured his instruments. For his chains he used reels of wire, a little thinner than coathanger wire, from which he cut two-inch lengths. He twisted each of these into a loop and then swung the ends forward and slightly down into a double claw which was then used to grip the loop of the next link. The chain could be worn twice a week from the time of rising in the morning until after breakfast. It was looped around the upper calf or the lower thigh, and the links and claws allowed for tighter or looser wearing. Too loose, however, and it could slide down the leg and out the trousers when one moved, notably at Communion time. This was a particular concern when there were Externs such as retreatants in the chapel. The claws dug into the skin and the red impress remained for some time after the chain was removed. The wire did not cut into the skin although fabled Tradesmen from the past were supposed to have taken a pride in sharpening the severed wire ends. Each novice received his own new chain and in our time the points of the claws were, in relative terms, quite blunt.

The Tradesman alternated chains with disciplines. The disciplines were small whips, made from delicately slim, white rope of superior quality. Six lengths were plaited to-gether for about six inches and were then allowed to run free as six tails for another twelve inches. The Tradesman re-versed the end of each tail and wound and knotted it around its own length until he had a small tight cylinder. He snipped the untidy residues of rope and sponged the whole of the discipline in resin so that it had a glazed, stiffened consis-tency, and he soaked the knotted cylinders in the resin until their tightness had shrunk to an unsqueezable hardness.

The Master of Novices gave me, as he gave each of us, a chain and a discipline when I had been a novice for about a month, and he explained their rationale in the Christian tradition. I was bringing my own body into subjection, I was uniting myself with the sufferings of Christ, I was offering up my pain as a compensation for my own sins and those of the world. This was theologically rich, even exalted, and I accepted the chain and discipline gladly. Just fifteen strokes, said the Master of Novices. No more. He said nothing about the time I might take or the vigour and ferocity with which I might administer the blows. On Wednesday and Friday nights, when we had all gone to the dormitory, the Porter opened his window on to the verandah and, reaching out his hand, he rang the *tocco*, a small reminder bell. So when I was undressing and had my back and chest, but no more, bare, I took the discipline. I tingled with life, arrested in my semi-nakedness, shrinking from the hurt but determined on substantial blows. I held my breath, and not just against my own pain. My nerves prickled through the thin floral curtains. I hung there for all the other flurries of strokes, the gasps, the brutal excess, the drawn-out counts, the soft tailing away. Throughout the small room, as near as four feet from my own body, I heard and measured the flail of the rope against the flesh I could not see.

We all registered force and volume, and inevitably it was adverted to.

"Brother Hackett," remarked Michael Finnane to a sympathetic group, "a most edifying pull on the rope. I'm sore just from hearing it."

I grinned and turned away, laughing. I said nothing. It was a Forbidden Topic.

The office of Tradesman was sometimes temporarily suspended when the stockpile of chains and disciplines became large enough for projected needs. In 1964 only ten novices entered, and a pattern of diminishing numbers was set. The twenty-three entrants of 1963 proved a high-water mark. Quite soon the office of Tradesman was redundant. Chains and disciplines ceased to be distributed. Penances were not spoken of.

In place of the old staples for our minds, we were introduced to new. Prescribed reading took up an hour and a half each day. For an hour in the first year of our religious life we read *The Practice and Perfection of Christian Virtue* by Father Alphonsus Rodriguez of the Society of Jesus. We also had a short excerpt from Rodriguez read aloud each evening in the refectory. The work was a product of the late sixteenth century, the translation only a little later, and its monopoly of our reading in ascetic spirituality was curious. But it was by a Jesuit and it was comprehensive, with treatises on numerous Christian virtues and habits. Humility, Obedience, Prayer, Poverty, Mortification, Charity … Each treatise contained a number of chapters, the last one always entitled "In which the Foregoing Doctrine is Confirmed by Divers Examples". I laboured, and sometimes dozed, through the arid expanses of doctrine, but I was buoyed by the prospect of anecdotal colour.

The Master of Novices handed out the volumes of Rodriguez and supervised the readings. "There are two treatises there you needn't bother with," he said. "Just skip over 'Chastity' and 'Relatives'."

I sampled the not-quite-forbidden treatises. The madcappery of the saints grew extreme. Men who had shaken off all other earthly ties had their chastity tempted by demons, demons who took the form of alluring women. Men thrust the demons away ruthlessly or they were themselves lost. Saint Kevin drove his demon to her death from his cave high above Glendalough. Saint Thomas Aquinas, a burly man, used a fiery brand to expel a harlot whom his worldly brother had introduced into his cell. Saint Aloysius Gonzaga, knowing how fragile chastity was, would not raise his eyes to the exposed flesh of his mother's face. Saint Francis Xavier, travelling through Spain on his way to board ship for the Far East and his eventual death, and passing near his birthplace and family home, made a long detour to keep at bay his mother and father and brothers and sisters. Saint Bona, the good woman, a widow, had a purulent breast. She accepted the affliction as sent by the hand of God, and when one of the maggots fell from her breast she bent down and lifted it back to be with its brethren in their designated home.

For the remaining half hour of our prescribed reading we had the saints to themselves unencumbered by doctrine. The period was called Life of Saint. The Master of Novices had eliminated the older examples of hagiography, and we read respectable biographies of men and women, often of figures not formally recognised as saints. We sat four by four at our desks along each wall in each camerata, each Life of Saint on its adjustable book-stand. Two lives went on there at each desk. The novice and the companion chosen for him mingled. My chair might creak slowly as I leant back in indifference or even boredom. Or I might turn the pages with brisk interest, caught up in another's life as I never otherwise was throughout my day.

It was storytime, the only one I had. I had committed myself, my life was as static and controlled as it is possible to be. Any major movements — where I lived, what function I performed — would be decided for me. The only story I imagined for myself was the sepia story of my soul. I threaded my way through the patterns in the lives of suggested companions. I was admiring or intrigued or sceptical or repelled. Airy models for my life floated up, floated past. I held and was held by inconse-quentialities and ironies. Odd loops snagged me. The saints caught my ear and hooked the nerve ends of my imagination.

Father Bernard Vaughan preached a series of sermons on "The Sins of Society" at the Church of the Immaculate Conception, Farm Street, in Mayfair, and attendance became so fashionable that the church overflowed. John Vianney, *le curé d'Ars*, spent up to nineteen hours of every day in the confessional and was in agony over the terrible volume of sin that was poured into his ears. When he took refuge in his own house with a few boiled potatoes and a couple of hours on the bare floor the poltergeists roamed freely, teasing him with their cries and spinning his meagre supply of crockery to the floor. Janet Erskine Stuart, convert and fifth Mother General of the Religious of the Sacred Heart, had an old titled Anglican aunt; "the best-dressed women I know," the aunt said, "are Janet's nuns." Willie Doyle, an Irish scholastic, did his philosophy in England during the Boer War; any news of a Boer success was Ireland's opportunity, and Willie Doyle stepped out of his room into the corridor and gave three loud cheers for the Boer cause. Father Michael Browne, novice master to the Irish province, spiritual father to saints and scholars, said that the most holy and exalted mystic he had ever known was a Dublin washerwoman.

I fastened on the saints and held them before me, excluding all others. I wanted them to clamber up out of the grave and stretch themselves and be seen again. When schoolboys came to Watsonia to do retreats we waited on them at table in their refectory, and we read to them there. I held up before them *Father William Doyle S.J.: A Spiritual Study* by Professor Alfred O'Rahilly.

There were perhaps six meals to get Willie Doyle across to the schoolboys, so his childhood, youth, years of training and study as a Jesuit were all skipped, and the boys joined him in the midst of it all, as a chaplain on the Western Front, writing home to his father. I read, and I felt the reading advance from one threat to another against the boys' apathy. Father Willie Doyle's favourite phrase was "brave Irish lads" and compulsively he compiled

statistics on Confessions heard and Communions administered
to the brave Irish lads of the Dublin and Royal Irish and Leinster
and Iniskilling Fusiliers before countless offensives or just pro-
bing thrusts. Father Willie Doyle talked of mud and stench and
the remains of poor fellows, recounted how he wrestled with a
gassed officer who wanted to throw away his mask, and
thanked God for the fortification he had been able to give his
poor brave lads. The boy retreatants lunged for their rissoles and
piled their sideplates with bread and hissed and whispered
volubly up and down their tables. At Third Ypres Father Doyle
spoke of rats and burial parties and of his movements between
the battlefield and the casualty stations and how he had had to
anoint a man whose face had been blown away and of how he
could not find an unblemished spot on which to lay his oiled
thumb. The retreatants turned unselfconsciously in their chairs
and stared at me as they chewed, and I read on through the
barrage of their stares and curiosity, and then they turned back
and whispered to the boys beside them and looked along the
table to see if there was anything of anything left in the dishes.
The priest conducting their retreat tapped me on the shoulder
and I had to cut Father Doyle off as peremptorily as he himself
had been by the shell that ended his life. The priest clapped and
the boys, still chewing, mumbled one or two words of the Grace,
then noisily pushed for the door and took off into the far wooded
corners of the grounds.

huc omnis turba ad ripas effusa ruebat ... A whole spreadeagled
crowd was making pell-mell for the banks. There were mothers
and husbands and the lifeless bodies of mighty heroes there,
small boys and unmarried girls, and young men and young
women whose own parents had had to watch them being placed
on the pyre. They were as numberless as the dead leaves that
flutter down in the forests at the first chill of autumn. They were
as countless as the birds who throng together when the turn of

the year drives them in search of a warmer habitat and they come beating in from high above the heaving ocean. All stood there praying to be taken first across the river, and their arms were stretched out in a terrible longing for that farther bank. But the grim troubled sailor just takes these ones, and then these ones, while all the rest he drives away and pins far back from the sandy edge.

My saints should have been, if anywhere, around me, there for the observing when I arrived at Watsonia. The old men of the Society of Jesus. I was told there had been giants in the house before my time. Father Sylvanus Newport was never without a brown paper hat to protect the one unclothed part of himself from things that fell from the noxious air. He had the largest room in the house and was favoured by some as a non-intrusive confessor, for he positioned the penitent's prie-dieu barely inside his door and he himself sat, facing away, shielded by a curtain, in the diagonally opposite corner. He was in every way careful and frugal and yet somehow splendid. He attended no community meals, but came down to the kitchen late at night to prepare himself some boiled vegetables. His sense of economy was both passionate and inventive; he drove by preference on the wrong side of the road in order that the tyres should be worn down evenly.

I never saw Father Newport but Brother Jimmy Madden, who had been in another era, passed across the stage for me. He had a beautiful oval head, smooth but for the barest white prickle on top. The finished plasticine of his lips rolled over any stumps of teeth that were there, and when he spoke his lower jaw, and only his lower jaw, moved rapidly like that of a ven- triloquist's doll and the grizzled voice sounded from some- where below his chin. While I was a novice Jimmy Madden came back to Watsonia to do the brothers' annual retreat. I was serving at dinner that week, and was seated at the bottom of the refectory at what we called Second Table with the other novices who had been serving and working in the scullery. Jimmy Madden padded in, his head taut and bobbing on his foreshortened neck. At his side was Leo Cussen, a fellow brother, deferential and companionable, and when Jimmy Madden saw the table full of the riches of new faces, he angled towards us. Leo Cussen's always present, always gentle ironic smile broadened just fractionally and he moved in to Jimmy Madden's elbow to make the introductions. We were on silence, but this was a member of our family we had not met before, and he was greeting us. Jimmy Madden moved along the sombre table, and his hand went out in greeting as Leo Cussen presented each of the novices to him. We half stood and turned awkwardly, and as we acknowledged our names and took his hand Jimmy Madden named a date. It was our birthday. We each gave a laugh of surprise and subsided slowly, watching the trick being repeated down the table. He made no mistakes, he never hesitated, he ventured nothing other than the dates. He reached the end of the table, and Leo Cussen with a wry smiling deference held open the scullery door. Jimmy Madden processed through and disappeared.

Father Newport, Brother Madden were men to marvel at. But it wasn't sanctity I was learning about from these revelations and visions. I looked around me at the men in the house now, and I was still baffled. Father Turner was an invalid. He looked all right and was mobile and had a good appetite, but he was said to have a heart. Apart from being a confessor he did nothing, nothing that I saw. Yet contact with him was regarded as desirable. Each week he had, alternately, a novice or a scholastic to attend to him. He slept in and said his Mass late in the morning. At nine o'clock his attendant went to his room with a glass of orange juice. Vic Turner was usually but not always dressed. He sipped the juice, as he did everything — walking, speaking — in the most measured way, and he had an epicurean habit of pursing his lips, not tightly, and popping them, very gently, while his tongue moved gravely on a constant round of inspection. The whole oral activity continued even when he was not drinking or eating. While he was sipping his juice we removed his urine bottle and emptied and washed it out and replaced it under a white linen cloth. Then we made his bed, and usually this was all done in silence because he was at prayer. At twelve o'clock he said Mass in a tiny oratory off the parlour where there were no steps to climb and no distances to be traversed. He was in the refectory for lunch at one o'clock, and in the afternoons he frequently went out. He was short and sharp-featured, with a small elegant paunch, and his clerical clothes were well cut and spotless. When he went out he drove himself. I was puzzled by him and never enlightened. He had been a chaplain during the war and had been a prisoner of the Japanese. I didn't know whether that made him a saint, or a fraud or what. But it must have done something.

In the personnel booklet, the *Catalogus*, that each province of the Society of Jesus published every year, a man's responsibilities were listed. If he were past responsibilities he was listed "*Orat pro Soc.*" "He is praying for the Society." As novices we found this phrase hilarious.

Father Eddie Carlisle was praying for the Society, but to my mind he was up to a lot else. He was an Englishman and convert and came to Watsonia from Sydney for his holidays. Not that he was doing any specific work in Sydney. He was elderly and very stooped, but he had a rubbery limp and a similarly agile stick. He had white hair and a pale, softly craggy face, and in spite of his infirmities he behaved like a voluble limpet. A generalised caution went amongst us — and I don't know whether it actually came from superiors or simply from past experience — that we were not to encourage Father Carlisle; this really meant not talk to him. His activity seemed to be defined by prohibitions. He was supposed not to do any phoning, and in particular he had been forbidden to phone Mr Santamaria. He was an admirer of Mr Santamaria, and he gave out that he was an intimate, but I never knew whether the embargo on his calls was initiated by cautious superiors or had been suggested by Mr Santamaria himself. Forbidden the phone, Father Carlisle went out. He armed himself with holy cards and miraculous medals, aids to piety that were already dating by this time. He eyed off suitable passengers on the train or the tram and he accosted them with his profession and the call of Christ. He distributed his pious objects and he preached the Gospel.

My real problem — because he was with us all the time and because I could not spot the saving grace, much less the sanctity — was Father Jimmy Dunne. Father Dunne had been at River-view in 1956 but all I could remember him doing was super-vising the Sixth Class boarders during morning study. At nine o'clock he pushed out, wordlessly and impassive, through the thronging dayboys waiting to get in. I couldn't say he had been retired to Watsonia because he had a job: he was the Econom. The word, dactylic but reverberating with the long O of the last syllable, was itself risible. Econom was a translation of *oeconomus*, more normally turned as bursar or accountant, but in Jimmy Dunne's case he was always the Econom. He was nothing else, certainly not a confessor. I had no idea what qualifications he had for the job, or how conscientiously and efficiently he functioned as Econom. But the title suited him. He was barely five feet tall, of freckled russet colouring, and he moved in a noiseless, almost insidious way. His most pointed feature was a hearing aid. He fiddled with it frequently, but whether to turn it up or down or in fact off, I didn't know. At some stage he had given up communication and had retired into a well-nigh solipsistic world. He did not go to the Fathers' recreation, he did not come to the refectory on occasions when talking was permitted. If the meal was thrown open unexpect-edly to talk, because, for example, a visitor was present, Jimmy

Dunne would sit in silence, almost motionless apart from the bare gestures needed to eat his food, and his neighbour would know not to broach a conversation. On occasion during his gliding passage through the day, he was seen to pause beside one of the brothers or a senior, less pious scholastic, and whisper. The words provoked a smile, but never a further response, for he moved on immediately. He never stood and talked. From his manner and from the response, I imagined these whispers were always somehow sardonic. He only ever whispered to me once.

He never went out. I never saw him out of his gown, in just his clericals. His room was in the front of the building, on the middle floor, and from just to the right of the central tower he could look down on the long sweep of the lawn. At work or walking in front of the property we could see the small knob of his head above his window ledge. Someone said that he had a hobby. He devoted all the time in his room to grinding lenses. No one knew if he had any practical purpose in this.

"His room must be full of them," I said. "All the time he has."

"Do you know how long it takes to grind a lens? One lens?"

"What does he want them for?"

No one knew what he wanted them for. His head moved above the level of the window and occasionally reared up. It was as much as I saw. In the room I imagined gnomish industry and a home that somehow contented him. But no one was ever in the room with him, and perhaps behind the walls all he was doing was grinding away at the unbreakable enclosure of his life. I had no idea.

One afternoon my family were visiting me, on one of the four permitted visits each year, and we were talking and eating cake and sipping tea and soft drink on the front lawn, thirty or forty yards from the building.

"Who's that man?" said my brother Michael, who was ten.

"What man?"

"That man up there."

"That's Father Dunne."

"What's he doing?"

"Shh, keep your voice down," said my mother.

"I don't know," I said. "It's all right. He's deaf."

"Why's he wearing his pyjamas?"

"His pyjamas! He's not."

"He is. Look."

"Don't all stare," I said. "He's not blind as well."

That evening I was coming out of the chapel after dinner. For the first and only time Jimmy Dunne slid beside me, and as he glanced off he said, "I was not wearing pyjamas."

Yet every evening the unambiguous saints were summoned in force. When everyone had finished his meal and the dishes had all been cleared away and the *Dux* of serving had bowed to the top table and left the refectory, the priest presiding at the meal called out, "Martyrology". In the pulpit at the far end the reader marked the place in the secular book and took up the heavy leather-bound volume that listed the saints. In the black and red lettering that is now used only for sacred texts the holy men and women were enumerated. In Latin the reader gave out the date, according to the Roman computation by kalends, nones, ides, as well as by day of the month and year. Then he started on the hagiology. Every day there was a legion of holy men and women dying and being done to death. Name, status in the Church — always in the genitive case for it was the feast of each one that we were marking — place of death. At the start the deathplaces read as a list of every recess of the Roman Empire, but then they spread across the world, the datives and ablatives of place spinning before us, teasing us to find the new world in the old, to see past the ancient patina to bright modernity. *Lutetiae Parisiorum, Cantuariae, Cordubae, Burdingalae, Vindobonae, Marrochii, apud civitatem Dunum in Hibernia, Carthagine nova in America meridionali, apud Auriesville in statu Neo-Eboracensi, in regno*

Maravensi apud Indos Orientales, Nangasachii in Iaponia, Paris,
Canterbury, Cordova, Bordeaux, Vienna, Morocco, Downpat-
rick in Ireland, Cartagena in central America, Auriesville in New
York State, Madura in India, Nagasaki in Japan. Across the
continents the witnesses to our faith departed this earthly life.
There was very little here that we were told about their lives; it
was their deaths, and frequently the violent circumstances of
their deaths, that we were recalling. The martyrology was sober,
but it had an eye for the more idiosyncratic deaths. I waited
every year for the epitome of these deaths, which also happened
to be an epitome of the Christian death, and I was miffed if I
were working in the kitchen or out of the house when this death
came round in April. He was only a lector and not even the
martyrology remembered his name and it happened during a
nowforgotten bloodbath somewhere in Africa. The Latin was
simple, and we gasped with the gurgle of delighted horror when
the reader finally told us that in the church on Easter Sunday,
the lector *"dum in pulpito ALLELUIA cantaret sagitta in gutture
transfixus est"*, and the coadjutor brothers, with their no Latin,
recognised the sound, "while standing in the pulpit and singing
the Alleluia he was shot with an arrow through the throat". The
moment however that the precise physical blow — of the arrow,
the axe, the rope, the brazier, the oil, the sword, the tomahawk
— lands and the brain occludes, the translation is effected and
no one dies. The eternal line of the figures in the martyrology
slip into rest in peace, or consummate their earthly course, or
migrate in glory from the world, or fly to their heavenly home-
land, or give back their souls to God, or fall asleep in the Lord.
All the metamorphoses of the crucified body flashed in succession from the pulpit above us. Unquenchable illuminations,
they stretched ahead of us. The reader capitulated to the myriad
blossoming of them. *"Et alibi,"* he called, "And elsewhere ...",
*"aliorum plurimorum sanctorum martyrum et confessorum atque
sanctarum virginum,"* "so many other saints, martyrs and

confessors and holy virgins." Before he had quite finished, the polyphony began. A hundred chairs were scraped back, a hundred bodies arose, adroit or laboured, and there was the ragged acclamation of wood striking against wood. Then these hundred other aspirants to sanctity stood in silent attention, waiting for Grace.

Over the Hills and Far Away

I realised early that we were ringed by institutions. The Watsonia Army Barracks lay south-east. If we went out to our south-west across Preston Paddock, and along the edge of a thin wood we could skirt Gresswell Rehabilitation Centre and Mont Park Psychiatric Hospital until we came to the site designated for Latrobe University. To escape encroachment we had to go north along the eastern boundary of the Christian Brothers' Training College until we reached the Maroondah Aqueduct and then we turned north-east across the Janefield Colony and so out into the open Plenty country. The most direct route there passed within sight of the Janefield buildings, and across the mucky softness of its home paddocks.

A resident of the colony was making his way in. He carried a bucket and a pitchfork. Our paths would meet, and in that case we were permitted to speak. Moreover we were aware we were crossing his land.

"Hello," we all said.

He stopped.

We gauged the lines and the limits of conversation with a resident of the Colony.

He put down his bucket and smiled at us.

"You've finished work?" we said.

His shoulders wriggled uncertainly.

"For the moment?" we said.

"Sort of." He was relieved.

"It's all dairy here, is it?" we said, being professional.

"Yeah. Cows," he agreed.

David Buckingham took a sweeping look around him. There were few animals in sight, but his glance took in the total, even invisible, holding. "And what do you use the bulls for?" he asked.

The resident's eyes skipped from one to another of us. He grinned but there was doubt in his expression; he feared a joke against himself. He bent his head, and with a blush across his grin, he mumbled "Oh fuckin' …"

I heard nothing more. But I could have sworn there was a rising inflection; he was not at the end of his sentence. He couldn't find the right answer. He was protesting at being teased.

We were as confused. David Buckingham jerked his hand out in protest, but left it hanging there, shaking, while his ribcage bounced with embarrassed guffaws. We laughed and we nodded and our eyes held David at arm's length, just as they patted and said thank you and backed away from the young resident.

At a quarter to nine on Thursday mornings we were given fifteen minutes speaking time to arrange the day's outing, or "villa". Villa spots were suggested, the names written on slips of paper and laid on a long table. Each of us held in his hand his own name peg, and juggled and tapped it while he considered the possibilities. Within the confines of time, charity and religious detachment, we tried to arrange, jockey, even exclude, but our pegs had eventually to be placed, name face down, under the slips of paper. Amidst all the jostling and the count-down to nine o'clock we could never distinguish all those up-ended identities; the pegs could not be lifted and read, and uncertainty about even your own peg once you had taken your hand away made second thoughts difficult. Besides, you couldn't be sure who had not yet chosen; you could not stop more people joining your own line.

There had to be at least three names under a locality for it to be viable; if there were only two of you, you were asked later, separately, which other spot you were willing to go to. Even if you had succeeded in having your name go down with a chosen companion's for the same spot, there was no guarantee that you would be in the same group for the all-important trek there and back. You could not travel in groups larger than five, and the Porter, the novice appointed for three months to run and record the noviceship's more humdrum affairs, arranged the groups. They were not to integrate or become muddled in transit. In any case the Master of Novices inspected the Porter's deployment, and if he wished to alter any venues or combinations he did so. When we came downstairs at ten o'clock, we checked the now-exposed, arranged groups, and we went where we had been assigned.

We spoke of "going on villa", "being out on villa". The term was derivative. Religious orders, or sometimes even particular houses of a religious order, were like wealthy urban dwellers from Roman times on; they maintained a recreational place in the country. So in New South Wales the Jesuits had a holiday house at Gerroa, on the northern end of Seven Mile Beach. In Victoria they had a former guesthouse on the cliff above Angle-sey. Most of the Jesuits in the country took a formal holiday at one or other of these places during January; this was known as the Major Villa. The term was used for the period and the holiday, rarely for the residence. For the most junior members of the Society, villa meant our outings every Thursday and on feast days. Villa on those days was invariable. Only when heavy rain had already set in at ten o'clock on a Thursday morning did the official notice appear on the board. "Rainy Day *Declaratur*," it said. We stayed at home and talked or played bridge or read.

When we went on villa at 10 a.m., we made for specific destina-tions. We could not just go walking or wandering. Occasionally we went south and south-east through built-up areas to parks in suburbs like Macleod or Heidelberg. Generally, however, the territory that had been staked out over the years was the unsettled country north-east of Watsonia bounded by the Plenty and Yarra Rivers. More vigorous and ambitious novices pushed beyond these confines to reach Yan Yean, Warrandyte, Hurstbridge, Kangaroo Ground. Within our own regular domain, more properly in the bush, we had our own nomenclature for the places we visited. Villa spots were occasionally identified by distinctive geographical features: Peninsula was a hump of land surrounded for 300 degrees by a twist in the Plenty: Chimneys was marked by the most durable ruins of an old cottage. Otherwise, spots bore the names of Jesuit saints. There were myriad spots and a man's Christian and surnames were assigned to separate places. So we had Gonzaga's as well as Aloysius, Kostka's as well as Stanislaus. The younger saints, those who had died at about our age, had clearly been most favoured, but even the more obscure Jesuit saints had been honoured. We went to Jogues', Spinola, Regis, Borgia's, Pignatelli's. All these names had been set in place before our time, and they seemed earnest, pious and predictable. But villa was not a day off from the pursuit of sanctity. It was simply the search by other means. We had to find time somewhere for the midday quarter hour examination of conscience and for the Rosary. We had to keep our sense of the presence of God, in the midst of continuous talk and laughter and physical exertion. We had to, as sooner or later we would constantly have to do as Jesuits, cope with the world beyond our own like-minded family. For all the raucous, carefree overflow of villa, it was also a first, protected step towards the apostolic life. So we had Jesuit saints scattered across the Plenty and Yarra basins, watching.

Yet these proprietary rights were beginning to look not quite so certain. For there was also a Pacelli's in existence before our arrival, and this move away from the Jesuits to a recent pope seemed imaginative enough, but perhaps also something of a

betrayal. We followed it up ourselves with a new
Roncalli's, although Pope John XXIII had only died
entered. This may have been the onset of frivolity, or at least of
insufficient reverence, for soon after, Michael Sullivan, a wag,
named a new location Ganganelli's after the Franciscan friar
who became Pope Clement XIV and suppressed the Jesuits in
1773.

The one anomalous, inappropriate name was Lulu's. She was
the sister of a man, now a scholastic, who had been a novice four
years before us. Lulu's was the spot where we had been taken
for our first villa. Where Michael Liston had drowned. We never
went to Lulu's again. We forgot where it was and, gradually,
even its name.

One Thursday in the spring of 1963 an uncommonly large group
of us gathered in the lee of a slope high above the Plenty. The
year was too far advanced for us to boil the billy. We drank water
taken from the Aqueduct and flavoured with powdered rasp-
berry cordial, and without the centre of a fire we lay and moved
around among the haphazard rockery. The river below us could
only be glimpsed in patches, but it was hidden merely by thin
scrub and the slight overhang of banks. Someone picked up a
small stone and hurled it towards the water. It disappeared
without a sound into the vegetation. Someone else selected, with
some care, a larger stone, and took aim. It flew, avoiding the
gauntlet of branches, and we saw it — and were sure we also
heard it — splash into the river. There was applause and a rush
to collect stones. Down they flew, span upon span. Yet no one
seemed able to repeat the consummated splash into the bright
water. Each stone came to grief in the net of branches and
clunked to a dead stop or skidded sideways out of its trajectory.

"Bugger this for a joke," said someone, and he picked up a
boulder the size of a small pumpkin, and making a sling of his
hands he swung his arms back between his legs and tossed the

rock forward. It travelled only perhaps five yards through the air, but landed on one of the sharper inclines and, unimpeded, it rolled on confidently. It came to a slight eminence and dropped over, but the ground below was hard and still steep and it bounced on, brutal and accelerating. We were all watching, and we laughed and we cheered as it broke away. Then, just as we thought it was unstoppable, it took a bounce out of the straight line of its course and thudded into an embedded wall of stone. It rebounded, dazed, and gave a gentle shudder, took a half roll and lay still. We grunted in chorus when it was struck, and gave a frustrated groan when it stopped. But the top of our hillside was dotted with every size of rock; we turned, each of us, for a new missile. We eyed up weight and strength and launch pad and slope and sent our rocks plunging. Success lay with mass, and there were boulders around us, perhaps five feet high, nearly as much in diameter, that the millennia had been silting up with their detritus. Engineers and overseers and labourers identified themselves in an instant. The eucalyptus sticks that we would have burnt in the wintertime, the knives for spreading our butter and jam, any sufficiently sharp and graspable piece of stone, all were put to use. Grubbing out was slow but we had all afternoon. The sun was moving away to our left and caressed our backs and shone into the concave hollows opening under the boulders. The stones were rearing with a clean new beauty. The engineers became intent on the balance and the lean. I scoured and polished round a base till we were ready to squeeze from the hillside our dark core of basalt. The engineer judged the moment, the strain was taken, the angle of the fall checked, the feet and grip readjusted, and the strength was applied. The great rock toppled. It lumbered and then plunged and sideswiped its lethal way into the Plenty. The water quaked and then settled and readjusted its flow. I turned to the next boulder.

Later, in the fading afternoon, I walked away from a cleared, pitted hillside. I felt exhilarated by the energy and effectiveness of it all. Yet simultaneously I was subdued by the elusive, irrational force that had swept over me. I never rolled rocks again.

In November 1976, long after I had left the Society, I stayed in Rome with some friends, a married couple and their three small children. The marriage was coming apart, but so quietly that I had no inkling of it. They were renting an apartment in the Venerable English College on the Via di Monserrato. The institution dated from medieval times, first as a hospice for English pilgrims making the journey to Rome, and later as a seminary for English priests preparing to work in the England of the Penal Laws. In 1976 it was still a seminary, but much of the space in the College was superfluous to its needs and apartments were leased. The Australian Embassy had taken an apartment as a residence for some of its officers. There were substantial pockets of secular life in this ancient ecclesiastical world.

One Sunday the family said they would drive me up to the College villa. It was high on a volcanic plateau and looked across Lake Albano to the papal villa at Castelgandolfo. The villa was unoccupied, and in fact rarely used because the students now went back to England for their holidays. The concrete swimming pool was stagnant, and I was shown pockmarks and chips out of the exterior walls that were a legacy of Kesselring's retreat in 1944. I stepped over the weed-broken terrace with the woman and she told me that on her last visit to the villa she had walked in the orchard with a friend and he had picked and offered her wild strawberries and she knew that he wanted to kiss her.

Villa, when we were novices, was nothing so oblique or withheld. Released, once a week, we rushed into the countryside and the balloons of talk burst out, swelling, from our mouths. Inside them the mad saints tumbled and sported on the rungs of the ladder of perfection, the biblical scholars wrestled with the shadows of the first and the deutero and the third Isaiah, and the evangelists, man and lion and bull and eagle, jostled for primacy; the Petrine supremacy was dissected by the bony fingers of Irenaeus and Ignatius of Antioch while the dextrous Pauline privilege was squared with the lumbering block of the *Ne Temere* decree. Rare creatures requisitioned our balloons and trod them helter skelter at one another.

On the ground beneath we flicked our wrists and the eucalypt twigs snapped. Or we raised our knees and the thicker wood strained and creaked and came apart with a sharp crack and a final tearing protest. We threw the sticks on to the fire, both carelessly and strategically. The smoke eddied up and our eyes smarted and we shuffled our places. We tossed and twisted our heads and above them the balloons bumped and staggered and melded together and elastic hernial lengths were squeezed out. New spirits danced into all these vacant playgrounds — the *mots* of Escriva de Balaguer of Opus Dei came weaving on the heels of à Kempis; top-heavy Dominicans and nimble Jesuits wrestled over their missionary activities and all the might-have-beens of China. Just now and again a balloon took football shape or strained with the friction of a 1955 Labor Party. But the world and all its distractions passed. We had too many figures of our own pressing from the wings. Suenens and Ottaviani and all the street-wise cardinals manoeuvring in Rome, feinted for a stranglehold; Pope Pius XII's amanuensis, Father Oswald von Nell-Breunning waved his admonitory letter, *Mit Brennender Sorge*, and Rolf Hochhuth and Hitler and Stalin and all their divisions, and then the Vatican and its legions of angels, rolled out across the steppes in our endless stock of balloons.

We piled up the brushwood around the billy. The water rose to the leap of the flames and hissed as the handful of tea landed on its bubbling surface. Above us the balloons kept bobbing, sometimes sliding together into one dense cloud that overshadowed us all, then at some whim dividing again, and again, so that the exuberant crush of them bounced from speaker to speaker, juggling and somersaulting their freight, the whole bursting taxonomy of the Christian centuries.

I Preach, But Not Myself

2 Corinthians 4.5

There was no pulpit in the chapel at Watsonia. The only pulpit we had stood at the bottom of the refectory, in the corner opposite the kitchen doors. No priest ever stood in it. Scholastics and novices read there, and once a year they preached there. The platform stood over two feet above the ground and there were no steps. To enter it you gathered the skirts of your gown and leapt, or you put your hand on the frontal shield and hauled yourself up.

We did not give a sermon from it during our first year. For at least twelve months we looked to our own souls and worked privately to acquire the skills of preaching. Every week, we had a half hour class known as Reading and another known as Tones, the latter specifically on the subject of preaching. The content of the two classes overlapped. Father Kurts, the *Socius*, took us for both. Conscious of his body, he padded along the verandah on the balls of his feet, his head held high, and his shoulders rolling themselves back in an athlete's tic. He brought one text to each class and he gripped it with an assertive muscular control. Every time he touched the book, the movement had a rubrical fullness to it. He sat at the table and opened the volume and smoothed the pages with the rotating flat of his hand.

"Loud and clear, brothers, loud and clear." He looked around at us, seated on benches and chairs along the side walls. "Loud and clear," he repeated, even more slowly, and he twitched back the boards of his book. He got up and strode down the room and placed the book in the hands of Vince Hurley. Then he walked back towards his desk, intoning as he went, "This is Saki, brother, Saki." He gave no other explanation or introduction. "Start off, Brother Hurley. From the beginning."

Vince Hurley was thirty-one, a Queenslander, a primary schoolteacher. He bolted nervously at the words. " 'My aunt will be down presently, Mr Nuttell,' said a very self-possessed young lady of fifteen; 'in the meantime you must try and put up with me.' " The excited bumble of Vince Hurley's voice smothered the sentence.

The *Socius* sat bolt upright, his lips drawn back. "This is the English language, brother. We must give it air." His consonants exploded and snapped with a long-suffering precision. "Again, brother. Read it again. 'The Open Window.' "

We never got through "The Open Window". As secular writing it was not to be found in our library, and we had no access to it.

More frequently the *Socius* brought a larger book. He sat over it at the desk, turning each page individually and flattening it before moving immediately to the next one. Then he spun it around on the table so that it faced towards us, he aligned it on an exact parallel with the edge of the table, and then he called out a name. A name and another name, but the same book, the same passages, time and again. "Brother Windsor."

I liked this. I came forward and gathered the book, a rare sort of publication, from the premier Catholic publishers, Burns, Oates and Washbourne of Westminster, the *Occasional Sermons of Monsignor Ronald Knox*. I held it high, but hardly had to look at the text. The *Socius* lowered his head and closed his eyes and slid his hands back over his skull. I began to proclaim. "Up then, gird thee like a man, and speak out all the message I give thee. Meet them undaunted, and they shall have no power to daunt thee. Strong I mean to make thee this day as fortified city, or pillar of iron, or wall of bronze, to meet king, prince, priest of Juda and common folk all the country through." I rang down the tone of my voice, and I said, "Jeremias, One, verses 17 and 18." Then I picked up again, and began in, "The other day, in a

curiously moving country church at West Grinstead, we laid to
rest, not without the tears of memory, an old and tired man." I
read on, my mind rolling with the sonorities of it. I was careful
to emphasise the *Socius*'s own pronunciations and when I came
to the man, Hilaire Belloc, I gave the accent in both words to the
second syllable.

"Thank you, brother," said the *Socius*. "Monsignor Knox is a
very learned man, but look at how simple, how simple." He held
out his hand for the book, and then smoothed over pages again,
and called, "Brother McEwen".

Terry McEwen gave his signature scratch to the side of his
head and strode like a relieving sentry to take the book.

"The title and the occasion, brother," enunciated the *Socius*.

"St Ignatius Loyola," read Terry McEwen. "This sermon was
preached at the Church of the Immaculate Conception, Farm
Street, London, on the Feast of St Ignatius, 31 July 1930."

The *Socius* threw his head back and kept it there, running the
tips of his fingers against the sides of his jaw.

"Then his son Judas, called Machabeus, rose up in his stead;
and all his brethren helped him, and all they that had joined
themselves to his father, and they fought with cheerfulness the
battle of Israel."

I arched my neck against the windowsill behind me, and
basked in the warmth of it all.

In the *Socius*'s book the panegyric seemed the paradigm for our
sermons. But in fact the panegyric was what we might have
called an Extraordinary Tone. Tones was a peculiarly Jesuit
usage, current since the earliest days of the Society. Tones were
sermons, under their stylistic aspect. The model for our sermons
was known as the Ordinary Tone. Every novice, for as long as
we knew, had had to learn this brief but complete sermon in free
time and then deliver it in Tones, without warning, and more
than once. Its name was rich in implication. It was the sermon,
or at least the epitome of the sermon, that would normally be

preached. Its core durability was heightened, in fact hallowed, by being to all sermons what the Ordinary of the Mass, the unchangeable part, was to all Masses. We had every extrinsic reason to believe that the Ordinary Tone was the essential preaching of the Gospel. If we were to follow the exhortation of Christ to go forth and preach the Gospel to every creature, the Ordinary Tone was where we began.

The *Socius* brought a wooden fruitbox to Tones. He positioned it at the far end of the room and tested it for stability and strength. He went back to his chair at the table and called out, "Brother Enright". Then he rubbed his hands vigorously over his face as though he were washing it.

I had been at school with Tony Enright. He had done a year's Law and then been a surprise entrant to the novitiate, twelve months after I had gone there. As he went to the box the smile on his face was made all the more apparent by his strained solemnity. I saw a gingery cheekiness in his expression as he steadied himself on his platform.

The *Socius* lowered his head and closed his eyes and slid his hands back over his skull.

"You are aware, my dear brothers," began Tony Enright, "how man having through his own fault incurred the displeasure of God by committing sin was plunged into the lowest depths of degradation and misery."

I watched his arms stretch out and down, and jerk at the nethermost pit. It was the invariable gesture. Then his index finger rose for a moment of intimate attention-seeking.

"Yet think upon, admire the goodness, the tenderness, the generosity of the Divine Redeemer of mankind! It was for thy sake, ungrateful and rebellious creature, it was to save thee that He deigned to come down from his heavenly Home, that abode of unspeakable bliss, where he receives the homage of the angels, the archangels and the whole heavenly court, too happy to serve him."

The gestures followed the dips and rushes of the text. Tony

Enright's arms tightened in denunciation, then soared and spread in cosmic awe. His right hand shot out and pointed to the crucifix on the far wall. I followed his gaze.

"Behold, Christian. Behold thy Saviour and thy Master how he has become a slave for thy sake! O infinite goodness, Lamb full of meekness! Who has thus forced Thee to cloak Thyself with our sins, to accept death in order to give life to us — to us thy ungrateful and miserable creatures."

I had to look down at the floor. It all seemed a bit too much. Or perhaps Tony Enright was a bit too much. He addressed the crucified Christ with a throbbing intensity. The words seemed to need that, but the result sounded histrionic. I could feel Tony Enright's grin somewhere above me.

"O Senseless Men! Men sunk in the sleep of sin. Do you not hear the voice of his prophet Joel crying aloud, "Blow the trumpet in Sion, Sanctify a fast, Call a solemn assembly, Gather together the people, Sanctify the church, Assemble the ancients, Gather together the little ones. O fatal sloth! O deplorable list-lessness! Why do you not awake from your unworthy lethargy? Weep for your sins! Weep for the iniquities of mankind! Utter lamentations and wailings."

The firestorm raged and darted. I looked ahead of me, straight across the room. Ray Gurry, his mouth open and his finger across his lips in apprehensive longing, stared up at the preacher. On one side of him Stan Hogan appeared to blench at the sound, his chin angling in to his shoulder, his hands held steady on his knees. There was no telling the effect of the sermon on him. But on the other side of Ray Gurry was Michael Sullivan. There was no denying a delight in mischief dancing up in his eyes. His diminutive, portly uprightness was wholly geared to withstand his own welling cackle. Past the windows behind them went two coadjutor brothers, Paul Schulze and Vic Higgs, wheeling the laundry trolley. They both gave in to temptation and forgot their observance of the custody of their eyes, and glanced in at us. Their faces registered just wry, mild amusement.

"But what do I say? Does the Greater Glory of God demand nothing more of soldiers and companions of Jesus Christ? Go! Run through the streets and the market places, the towns and the country, summon the whole people to the great, grand work of saving their immortal souls."

I looked up for the peroration.

"All the men and the women ..." proclaimed Tony Enright. With his eyes on the lowered head of the *Socius* he bent and stiffened his arm, as he spoke, and suggested men. Then he rolled both arms, sketchily, sinuously, and suggested women.

Ray Gurry's one finger became the palm of his hand across his mouth. Behind his screen I could see the silent, controlled titter. My own eyes widened and I felt the possibility of a smile pass across my face. I knew this went beyond the rhetorical flourishes allowed to the preacher even in such a theatrical piece as the Ordinary Tone.

"... the great and the lowly, the young and the old," continued Tony Enright, his arms passing beyond gesture into a mime of his words. "Do you not see the multitude rushing headlong to perdition and Hell opening wide its abyss to engulf them? Go! Set the whole world in flames with the fire of Divine Love. It is at this price that God promises you His Grace in this life and everlasting happiness in the next."

It was so hard to hear the Ordinary Tone as something fresh. No amount of athletic presentation could make it so. Staleness was not the only problem. The Ordinary Tone was doctrinally solid, scripturally rich, it was comprehensive — the Fall of Mankind, the Incarnation, the call to the evangelical vocation, eternal life. But I sensed an excess to it, and I was not quite sure where this lay or what the contradiction meant.

The *Socius* brought his head up slowly, his eyes still closed. "Thank you, brother. Stay where you are a moment."

Tony Enright shifted his feet as far as his platform would

allow him. His smile withdrew just a little further into the background, and he took on the more humble solemnity of the soul awaiting sentence.

The *Socius*, still faceless, paused, sorting out his pairings. "Brother Hogan," he aspirated loudly.

Stan Hogan gave a start of surprise, stood up and crossed his hands in a butterfly in front of him. His gown sagged sideways from his rounded shoulders. "Well," he began, and the tone was considered, "Brother Enright stood up very well on the box. He knew the Tone well. Extremely well." Stan Hogan stopped.

The *Socius*'s face popped up, his eyes spread artificially wide. "Anything further, brother?"

"Ah … Brother made plentiful use of gestures." Stan Hogan stopped again, definitively.

"Brother Curran," called the Socius.

Stan Hogan sat down. Fred Curran hunched to his feet. His face was furrowed, a puzzled, melancholy half smile. He had nothing on the tip of his tongue. The *Socius* gave him time. "Brother's delivery was very confident," Fred Curran said eventually.

There was a long pause. Fred Curran hesitantly decided he could sit down. The *Socius* dropped his face away again. We waited. We did not make comments unless we were asked. We preferred to be charitable and encouraging. We never adverted to the matter of the Tone.

In the second year of the noviceship every novice preached one sermon from the pulpit in the refectory to the whole community. Subject to approval we chose our own text and interpretation.

I had eighteen years of sitting in the pews to guide me, and I had the *Socius*'s models of what you did with words when you stood up confidently on a box. It was the first time it had been given to me, as a novice, to put words together, on paper, and have them communicated. Since I had entered I had not read fiction. The only poetry I had read was in Latin, or translated from the Latin. The Socius had given us an unfinished story and a series of panegyrics. We went via "The Open Window" to the brothers fighting cheerfully the battle of Israel, to the old and tired men. The razzle-dazzle and the subsidence of all God's children.

Christ like us in all things, sin alone excepted, was the gospel I wished to preach. Illumination, not didacticism. The gospel was my literature and my poetry. I saw it fresh and uncontaminated — God incarnate, sweet-breathed and rank as any character from fiction. The find of my own life, not overlaid or obscured by two millennia and the world's rendering of him.

I chose the death of Lazarus and Christ's grief. At lunch on Monday I stood beside the pulpit during Grace. As everyone else sat, I sprang up and tapped the microphone. I held tightly to my pause till the diners had all settled themselves for the meal and had taken in my presence and the trollies had swung in. I waited till the lids had been lifted from the crocks of mince and the beefy reek had stabilised. Then I announced my text from the thirty-sixth verse of the eleventh chapter of Saint John's Gospel. "Jesus wept," I said with all the controlled drama I could project.

We were only absent overnight from the noviceship for one purpose. We did not go away for holidays. Even when we went on long bus excursions — to Daylesford or Lake Mountain or Point Wilson — we returned at night. The noviceship was the only place we slept, except for one month in the twenty-four that we were novices. We went to Caritas Christi, the hospice for the dying at Kew, and we worked and ate and slept there for twenty-eight days. The exercise was called Hospital Experiment. A novice was sent each fortnight and joined one who had already been there for a fortnight. I was sent on Sunday, 13 October 1963 in my first year. The Rectress, Mother Leo, supervised us. Her elderly assistant, the hospice's long-ago founder, Sister Chrysostom, prayed for us and gave us sweets when she thought she was unobserved. We worked in the men's ward and its pan room, not in the women's ward or the private rooms. We did whatever unskilled things we could do for the dying.

The first man I saw die was in his thirties. He was married and had children and was a migrant from central Europe. I learnt none of this from him. He had a brain tumour, and when I arrived he was already somewhere else, in the turmoil of his agony. He was a yellow, shrunken man, a tiny specimen pinned against the taut white of his bed. Arms, legs, skull, hairless torso all hugged one another. I stood back from the bed and looked and wondered about the man inside this animal. Even when I sponged him and changed his sheets and his clothes I hardly knew what sort of creature I had in my hands. The heat and the chilly run-off and the eyes clamped shut on the world gave me nowhere to manoeuvre for his comfort or my own. Breath was what I fastened on, the desperate skewings from one rhythm to another. But it was not a rhythm. Breath was tugged and dropped and then ran its own haphazard way until another attempt could be made to seize it. I watched the distended shaven head and I could do nothing. I wanted some hopeless coaxing plea to be made to this unreliable air that worried at him. But I was silent. I moved away, to other agonies.

Mr Hodgkinson bellowed from his further corner. "Nurse, Brother, get me a pan will you. Quick!" He called urgently and without shame. And frequently. We learned not to be panicked by the desperation in his voice. We pulled the curtains around him and set him up on his bed and could forget him. He laboured loudly and bitterly, and let us know the same way when he was done. "Brother, Nurse, take this pan away will you." The pan was empty. "Fucking wind. Just fucking wind," he cursed. Mr Hodgkinson had two daughters nuns and they visited him, but he would not be comforted.

Mr Portelli had been assigned the first bed to the right, just inside the entrance to the men's ward. His bed had become a cot, for the guard rails were permanently in place. He was blind and he spoke little English and he lay supine, without a single pillow to prop him. On the table beside him there stood a cylindrical green cardboard box. "Brudda," Mr Portelli called when I passed near him — and it was a soft gentle request — "Kool Mint". His breath tapered long on the word Kool and he could not disengage from the l without clipping it with an "a" sound.

"Certainly, Mr Portelli," and I wrapped his outstretched, quivering fingers around the small white egg of a sweet.

"For you, brudda," he called before he put the Kool Mint in his mouth. His eyes strained up in solicitude.

"Thank you, Mr Portelli, I will," and I rattled the box and checked to see how many were left, and perhaps took one.

Otherwise Mr Portelli never spoke to us or to the nurses. No novice had ever been to Caritas when Mr Portelli was not there.

His mind seemed unaffected. No one knew what was killing him — or even whether he was specifically dying at all.

Father Albert, an old German Pallotine priest, was the chaplain, but he was a patient too. He shuffled about in slippers and a check dressing gown but underneath he always wore his clerical clothes. The novices had to keep an eye on Father Albert. He had found his way to Caritas after a lifetime in the Australian desert among Aboriginal people. But now he lost himself at Mass, and even at Benediction, wandering up and down the ritual, unable to thread his way through the labyrinth of good news, self-immolation, and glory. We novices gave the right responses to the wrong prayers, led Father Albert by the arm, pointed and hastened him towards the end of this mystery. We knew nothing of him. A nurse took my photo with Father Albert. I stood apart and slightly behind him, like a minder.

We had other religious duties. We went to the office at midday and turned on the PR system throughout the hospital and recited the Angelus. Then we said five decades of the Rosary. Those of the patients who felt like it were invited to join in. Otherwise, we told them, they might like to listen prayerfully. At the end of the Rosary the novice who was leading the recitation that day made the triple invocation, "Agonising Heart of Jesus ..." and three times the other novice and those of the patients who felt like it answered him, "Have pity on the dying". When it was my turn I leant in to the microphone and tried to put on the words a spin that was heartfelt and not maudlin, generalised but directed to whoever wanted the personal blessing. The words spun away from me and bounced haphazardly through the wards and private rooms.

Mr Rayner sat sharp upright in his bed, and his hands scrabbled endlessly over and under the sheets. He was not a Catholic and he had no time for our prayers. His face was seamed under a shock of white, wiry hair, and his eyes were fired with permanent flecks of distraught red. He muttered, just below audibility, and we went over to find what he needed. His fist shot out and the unaware or the forgetful reeled under the cold bony blow. Mr Rayner's hand retracted and the fingers opened out, and in a splayed, arthritic way he scratched savagely at his scalp. His nails were long and grubby because no one was able or willing to clip them. "Dandruff, dandruff," he repeated with a tight, bare-toothed malevolence, and he tore in a sharp flurry at his head. Dandruff fell; something would have had to under his assault.

"What's the cure for dandruff? For dandruff, Brother?" and he stole a quick, direct look.

"I don't know, Mr Rayner," I said. "I don't think there is one."

He glared, and his hand slowed down and then slid underneath the sheet. He began a lingering scratch of his scrotum, and his face relaxed briefly before again hardening as the activity of his fingers became more a movement of traction than a simple flick of the nails across venous skin.

"Itchy balls, brother," Mr Rayner said. "I've got itchy balls."

I could see that.

"What's the cure for itchy balls, Brother?" he asked.

I had no idea.

"Do you get itchy balls, Brother?" Mr Rayner asked. The dry malevolence of his expression was unchanging.

We got away from Caritas on Sunday afternoon. We were told we had to go out. We could go in any direction we liked, but we went south-west down the hill through the outskirts of Kew and across the Yarra by the Collins footbridge and under the Skipping Girl's rope and so into the city. Dr Mannix had walked that way for years. His residence was next door to Caritas, and if we began from where he did, there was a symmetry in finishing where he had, at St Patrick's Cathedral. We had money for a milkshake, but otherwise we were not to stop or go into shops or houses. Only one type of spontaneous, unscheduled stop was possible and the rule applied to us always. Whenever we left Watsonia — on villa or to see a doctor or dentist — the only call we could make on the way was at any church or chapel — Catholic church or chapel.

We were given one other excursion during Hospital Experiment. Dr Mannix was ninety-nine and never left his residence, Raheen, but every month as a mark of his especial favour towards the Society of Jesus he met the two novices then working at Caritas. On the second Thursday of my spell at Caritas, 24 October, I went next door for half an hour to visit him. He received us in his bedroom, but he sat in an armchair by the fire fully dressed, wearing a biretta and with a tartan rug across his knees. I was eighteen, from Sydney, and politically naive. Paul Cleary was twenty and from the Clare Valley in South Australia. We sat on straight-backed chairs on the other side of the fire, but close-in, and we were constrained and deferred to one another as we introduced ourselves. I had never been in the presence of such age and I did not know how you spoke to such a slow-motion jaw and such slack-muscled eyes. I had no idea how age combined with eminence and how together they were approached. Nor had I ever taken on board any details of the life of this motionless, enduring shadow. We said Yes, and Well, to questions about the work at Caritas and the health of the Novice Master. We said nothing of God or the Vatican Council or the work of the Society. We said Yes, we liked Melbourne, but it was different. Colder. I looked at the high-stoked fire.

"Summer's nearly here though now," I said.

"Well the football's certainly over," said Paul Cleary. "We can all be reunited by cricket now." He rocked with a short nervous laugh.

"The English team will be here soon," I said. "The Duke of Norfolk's their manager. It seems a funny job for a duke."

Dr Mannix revolved the slack flesh of his lips and jaw.

"He's a Catholic, isn't he?" I said.

"Oh most certainly so," answered Dr Mannix with low sibilant assurance. He bobbed his chin up and seemed to go through a brief chewing motion. "I met his father, grandfather, ooh great-grandfather, anyhow now, one of them, a Duke of Norfolk at all events."

I leant forward on my chair and tensed with attention.

"It was in Rome, I was just a young, newly ordained priest. Another young priest and I were to have an audience with his Holiness, Pope Leo X111, but for some reason now I forget, we missed out on it." Dr Mannix paused, and his mouth moved as though he were trying to catch there the lost reason.

"The Duke of Norfolk, this fellow's ancestor, was in Rome at the time. He was leading a party of English Catholic pilgrims. He came to see me. He said he'd heard about the two young Irish priests who'd missed out on their papal audience. He invited us to join his party. Said he'd be delighted if we would."

Dr Mannix paused and his fingers on the rug slowly retracted into the fist. He turned his head and shoulders slightly as though he were shifting in his seat.

"That was very kind, very decent of him," I said.

Dr Mannix's tongue showed briefly. "We said no. We said no. We declined his offer."

I was unable to look into his face. His tone was measured, long-ago detached, but I felt embarrassed, even scandalised. I gave a quiet, meaningless snort.

Dr Mannix leant forward, no more than an inch, and his fingers uncurled themselves and both hands lifted for a moment free of the rug. "Ah but you must understand," he said, "that the English and the Irish weren't such good friends then as they are now."

"No, no," I said, and Paul Cleary chuckled.

A priest, the secretary, ushered us out.

I had one other unanticipated excursion before I finished at Caritas. Just before three o'clock on Tuesday, 5 November, I was going through the men's ward from bed to bed.

"Gatum Gatum, Mr Hodgkinson," I said. We'd had no broadcast, there were no radios beside the beds.

"Eh?" said Mr Hodgkinson, surprised at being addressed.

"Gatum Gatum won the Cup, Mr Hodgkinson. Do you think your daughters might have had something on it?"

Mr Hodgkinson was silent and didn't bother to look up.

"Gatum Gatum, Mr Rayner," I said, keeping my distance.

"Gavan Duffy?" glowered Mr Rayner. There was an old priest, Fr Gavan Duffy, in a private room down the corridor.

"No, Mr Rayner. Gatum Gatum won the Cup."

"Gavan Duffy? What sort of a name is that?"

Sister Chrysostom shuffled busily into the ward. Her Rosary beads and the linen of her habit grated together in agitation. "Brother, Brother," she called, and her little finger curled and shuddered. "Dr Mannix has had a bad turn. They need you in there. Go in the back way, by the kitchen door. The housekeeper will let you in."

We strode away, bright with purpose. Paul Cleary, a short man, had been replaced by Jim Kilbride, a rangy, insouciant dairy farmer from New Zealand. Neither of us was Dr Mannix's own. He was in his chair again, but his biretta was on the floor, and his hair fell in disarrayed wisps across his face. His eyes were closed and his head hung and his mouth was open and dribble crept from the corner of his lips. The secretary and Mother Leo leant in on either side of him. We were needed to get him into bed. Jim Kilbride took him under the arms, around the chest, and while the secretary and I did little more than keep the feet off the ground Jim Kilbride hoisted the old man, took several firm, balanced, steps backwards, then lifted himself into a kneeling position on the broad double bed. We backed across the expanse of coverlet till he could lay the unconscious man in the middle. I followed him up, holding the shanks together under my arm and swung them centre to fit with Jim Kilbride's sense of what was fitting.

It was all we were needed for. We let ourselves out. At Mass in the convent chapel the next morning the oldest nun, tiny Sister Audeon, who had given herself licence for a little freedom, came up to us and whispered, "Keep saying your prayers. Dr Mannix is still with us. He's holding his own. Ask Our Blessed Lord now to spare the dear old man a little longer." He died that afternoon and four days later I went back to Watsonia.

Every second Sunday night a novice returned home from Caritas. He would come down the stairs outside the Conference Room while we were having coffee after dinner. We jumped up when he came into the room, and when he had risen from saying his prayer we asked him, "How many?"

He gave a number.

We wowed, or we grunted in sympathy. His predecessors at Caritas called out names.

"Died yesterday," the homecomer answered. Or, "No, he's still alive," he might say. "Doesn't seem to be getting any worse."

We made whistling sounds of incredulity.

I felt disappointed, let down by Hospital Experiment. Only three men had died while I was there, whereas double figure mortalities in the space of a month were common. I had laid out no one. I had wheeled no bodies to the mortuary. I was quite unplaced in the competitive tallying we worked among ourselves. The failure had its edge only because I sensed I had missed the point of the experiment. Somehow, I believed, the proper spiritual fruit of the month lay in the deaths. I had not had them. I feared a softness in my soul. I had not looked long and hard and often at our last end. My perspective on everything was still unbalanced.

The Lifeless Bodies of Great-Souled Heroes

Aeneid VI, 306

We left our letters, unsealed, outside the door of the Master of Novices. I have no idea whether the Master of Novices read them at all. Maybe in the beginning. Maybe he just sampled. He was a sane and busy man and I doubt whether any inspections were more than cursory. But I don't know. Doubtless the desired effect was achieved. We wrote with a censorious readership in mind.

The Master knew the way the mind of a novice should be developing. The very action of entering religion meant that I was already well disposed. There were, however, the refinements of spiritual right-mindedness that had to be picked up. Every mountain lowered, every valley filled, all the rough ways made plain. A novice's temperament might make practice difficult, but there was no intellectual bucking against the shape and features of the designated perfect man. I bent my attitudes towards the mould that I knew they were rightly destined for. I wanted the right spiritual disposition, and I knew that what I wrote would be the litmus test, and that Father Master might well read me there.

It was my family I wrote to. They were the only ones I was allowed to write to. I wrote to reassure them that I was well and happy. Otherwise I was unsure what to do in my letters. I was not in my family's world any more. What was the fitting subject and the right tone? Were the letters to be about my life or an obscuring of my life? What was there to relate from an enclosed life, a routine governed by bells as frequent as five minutes apart? My prayer life and my resolutions to virtue I myself ruled out of bounds. I scratched for matter. I commented on the incoming correspondence. I corrected my brothers' grammar and spelling. I exhorted them to more frequent letters. I said I was glad to hear about their sporting successes, but added that there was another, more important, field of achievement. I detailed the arrangements for my family's visits to me. When I managed something from life at Watsonia I retold episodes from the books being read aloud in the refectory. *The Long Walk* by Slavomir Rawicz, *With God in Russia* by Walter Ciszek, *Jerusalem Journey* by William Prescott, *The Sky Beyond* by Sir Gordon Taylor, *The Shadow of His Wings* by Gereon Goldman, *Collision Course* by Alvin Moscow, *The Edge of Tomorrow* by Tom Dooley, *So We Take Comfort* by Dame Enid Lyons.

The pen ran free on just a handful of occasions. On 19 June 1964, for example, when I was nineteen and a half, I told my family how I was teaching catechism at Norrisbank State School. One of a pair of novices, I took a bicycle out along Grimshaw Street, riding north-west and skirting the ice-covered puddles that lay along the edge of the unguttered road.

> Of the five I had last week, two were aged four and couldn't write, read, spell or draw and consequently somewhat handicapped the whole class. A third child aged six was quite incapable of keeping still or keeping quiet and was the type who insists, more through fun, I think, than ignorance, on this sort of thing; "Who made the world?" "Luthifer." "Who was the leader of the fallen angels?" "Adam". The trouble is that he gets all the others mixed up. It's all quite an experience and something of a challenge.

I have no recollection of this boy. But I retain a sharp memory of a little girl. I was disconcerted by her prettiness. She had opulent black hair, and was uncooperative in a giggly, teasing kind of way. I understand it now; the boy was acting up for her, she was responding, and there was a flirtatious conspiracy between them. I stood on the raised platform, and she sat at a front row desk by herself, immediately beneath me, and I could not get her to look at me.

So what was the experience? The intractability of a six-year-old boy? The unsettling, unbiddable beauty of a five-year-old girl? (About which of course I said nothing to my family.) I cannot answer the question. I only ever recorded this one episode. I have no idea in what way I thought, at the time, I had been broadened by this lesson. But it was worth retelling to my family. Perhaps it was apostolic activity, the reason for which I had left them. As well as that, it was out of my routine, it was unpredictable, and it was a problem that I knew I had not solved.

The letters betrayed none of that. Yet, three years later, in May 1967, when I was a scholastic, it was still the unresolved that was pushing me into expansiveness.

A week or so ago I was coming back from voting at the local state school (as always) with two other schols. We were circling an oval when some of us, not me, saw a motor bike headed in our direction at about 30 m.p.h. and rather out of control. Luckily it passed safely but had barely done so when (and this I saw) it hit a bump and went up in the air. Luckily, again, bike went one way, rider another.

The latter, a boy no more than twelve, was unconscious. We got his helmet off and put him into a car that had arrived. To cut a long story short, we got him, via the young chap doing a locum at the local G.P.'s, to the Austin Hospital at Heidelberg. I don't think anything was broken because I had to hold onto his threshing legs and arms, but he was at least shocked and perhaps concussed, as he vomited, including blood, in the car.

I can see and smell it. I have always been able to, although I had quite forgotten the circumstances. The vomit was creamy, the size and texture of the organs of small animals; the blood was large clotted globules. It had a sweet odour to it. Or so it seemed, for any distaste or apprehension was quite lost in the excitement of the moment. A break from routine, an involvement in the lawless dramas of the world, a sensation of usefulness. This was urgent and elemental, and the effect was exhilarating: the nostrils caught only what was intoxicating in the atmosphere. I had no idea what became of the boy.

The only fuel that could be turned into any kind of brightness in my letters seems to have come from these detonations of chaos. I observed them, from my distance. On 30 January 1968, as many as five years after I had entered the Society of Jesus, I was able to say to my family of a day at the beach at Seaford:

> We had an enjoyable day, talking and so on, only spoilt somewhat for me by my coming on, during a run along the beach, a boy of ten who had been found floating in the water. Some chap (not the parents who arrived about ten minutes later) was trying mouth to mouth r. I ran for a doctor, rang one, but he was engaged in stitching someone and couldn't come, finally got lifesavers, then an ambulance arrived, and I left, the crowd by this time around ignoring directions by police etc to disperse. — I read in the paper next day that the boy was dead on arrival at hospital. There was no surf at the beach, quite a lot of people around. Same old story.

What was the point, when I was already twenty-three, of the languid insouciance of "spoilt somewhat for me"? I hardly made a case for the day that was spoilt — the best that I could say for it was that it was "enjoyable, talking and so on". The spoiler clearly was what made my day.

What same old story did I know? What story did this death retell? That we die unregarded? That in the midst of life we are in death? That carelessness costs lives? That you can never trust the sea, even at its most apparently placid? That parents are irresponsible? That parents are the most vulnerable creatures on earth? Or that I skipped off, that I could not see something through to the end? That I did not know how death and a day at the beach could be summed up together? That I was held in a kind of thrall — running along the waterline after all, clearly by myself — that restrained me from any more intimate perseverance?

Running, running. Revving the pace, turning up the heat. But a controlled exercise. Running nowhere. Running to the arbitrary, pre-determined point, turning and running back again. I only recorded one break in the dispassionate order of our lives. On Thursday, our routine day off, 10 March 1965, only a month after I had taken my vows and finished the novitiate, I was on villa at Peninsula, lying on my back, chatting fitfully with Michael Healy, when I saw the brown smoke rise from behind the hillock across the water. We ran the two miles home to Watsonia. "We were told," I wrote to my family, "that we could go and hitch a lift and do anything we could to help."

It was the anarchy of fire. Barely allowed, normally, outside the grounds, every quarter hour of each of our days accounted for, and here we were now being thrown out by our superiors into the local inferno, and not wanted back until the devil had been stopped. Did they really believe there was such a need for every able-bodied man? Were they concerned for the image of the place, a known stockpile of fit young males, if they did not lend out at a time of local danger? Was there some notion that the experience would do us good? What good? Were they themselves in some curious way overcome by smoke, sent into a delirium of irresponsibility? Were they throwing up their hands and letting the chaos of hell stage a rehearsal in their domain? For our being sent on this mission was anything but an obvious move. We were given no instructions, no equipment, no money, just sent out to deal with a burning world as best we could and as we thought fit.

An army captain from Broadmeadows picked me up at the gates. He was responding to a call, he said, from some "lasses" whose house was ringed by smoke. I went where the captain went.

> There was a road running around the top of a hill. There were a lot of houses on one side of the road and the fire was coming up the hill on the other side. The general idea was to stop it at the road. There were truly hundreds of people there, a lot of them with what they call knapsacks (tin cans full of water, with sort of pump hoses on them, which they wear on their backs), a lot with bags on the end of poles (beaters) and some with just bags. I pulled down a young tree with lots of greenery on it, but some fellow worker gave me a bag fairly soon after we started to work.

The fire looked fairly fearful coming up the hill but I think we stopped it through sheer weight of numbers. There was plenty of heat around; we put sopping handkerchiefs over our mouths and in a minute or two they were pretty well bone dry. Walking around on the burnt ground was pretty hot on the old feet too. We were out from about 5.30 and did not get home until 12.15 a.m. We spent most of the night riding around in various cars, trucks etc. to different fires or pseudo-fires, drinking free bottles of Cottees lemonade which were being distributed by the manufacturers, visiting, together with all sorts of other odd-bods, fire-threatened private houses, and occasionally helping to put out a fire. We met quite a few interesting people, and saw many that weren't sober, and did, I think, some useful work.

I heard 16-20 houses were destroyed in that area.

It was military life. It was the vocation we had been summoned to. We had been called to *militare sub signo crucis*, to service under the standard of the cross. To go where we were most needed, Ignatius said, and at an instant's notice. It was our first campaign, and it ran true to our instruction. The soul, we had learnt, is coddled early in its spiritual career. The masters of the spiritual life warned that the delight the novice derived from his early advances was a cud for the hungry slog of the years ahead. We went out to a fire which we smothered easily, and we lived gaily off the land, and we were a part of a numerous brotherhood which turned its force easily and devastatingly against any threatening breakout.

This was war. You stood on higher ground, you had your comrades in line to right and left, you watched the enemy also in line advance towards you — the Imperial Guard, Pickett's Division ... You held your fire. You were waiting until the action could be personal, until you could see the whites of their eyes. You had plenty of time in which you simply looked straight ahead and watched. You could do nothing to distract yourself from the shouts and screams and already entered-upon surge of pandemonium through your own head. You let it roll on to the rear of your eyes and your attention. You waited and you hoped. The central experience was this standing at my post, gazing at an assault developing, holding firm as the swelling roll of it beat on. So the fire rolled up to us, and we took a pace forward and closed with it. All along the line the swift heavy downthrust of the beaters and the breathy pumping of the siphons, and the fire writhed and expired.

To my family I was severely factual. The blandness of my letters told them of the order of my life. There was no tremble of disruption to my words. The disorder had come and had been swept away. Yet the ease of it unsettled me. This disorder had never really threatened me, and then, when I drafted myself in to stop it, it crumbled and disappeared. To remain so unscathed by battle? Not when the enduring struggle was to be with principalities and powers, and I knew that their fire, always exploding across ground of its own choosing, was never quenched. Furthermore, the grand scale of such a picture was a con. I was training for single combat, and largely in private. It was with an enemy whose face I was forever running and straining and grappling to see; who might even come up the hill towards me, his white handkerchief wiping the perspiration from a beaming, comradely face. I would have to look at him, long and intent, and trace the cast of the features and feel where malevolence lay and where human kindness. I knew too that in the gleam of any full-lit face I would also see myself.

There was no illuminated face in my letters. There were no features I stared at sympathetically and uncompromisingly. There were no names. I identified no fellow firefighters, none of the "interesting" people I met. For ten months after I began writing to my parents I did not mention any other novice. I referred, where necessary, to senior members of the Society of Jesus. Always by their titles.

My family said my letters were boring,

I was indignant. "It's all very well," I threw back at them, "but you've got the whole world to build your letters from. I've got only this place."

Even that was not true. I handed over my letters unsealed so that the Master of Novices could check on the soul developing. He needed to see it, not hardening, but growing ever more muscularly supple by the tolerance of charity. I have only this place, I said, but in fact I had very little of this place. Its people, I felt, were barred to me. To write about my colleagues, I sensed, would inevitably offend against charity or discretion. I could mention their virtues but I doubted whether my family would be interested in the terms of praise I would use. My heart wasn't in it. I wondered, fleetingly, how interested I was myself. It was a handicap to be able to say nothing of the people with whom I lived, the only people I ever really saw.

There was no capturing them in any other way. No novice had a camera, no one else took photos of the novices. Only my parents when they visited me, and they snapped me as a member of that family I now belonged to only fitfully and remotely. Other parents must have done the same for their sons. But we were never with our fellows. We were always in the unpatched, unfaded Visitors' Gowns that were borrowed just for this occasion, caught for the album in the home we had left, not belonging there or elsewhere, and our personalities camouflaged.

Yet there were fifty-five novices when I first entered, and we might have had a uniformity of purpose, but otherwise our personalities burst out far beyond our predictable range. The companionship was relentless, far more intimate and unrelieved than any marriage except that of the fettered old. So that when we emerged silent from meals, and had knelt on the floor of the recreation room and said the "Hail Mary", we rose up into a sparky friction of characters that made the noviceship a shimmer of colour.

Even in the silence faces were lifted up and dazzled. Near the end of the first week of the thirty day retreat, whilst we new novices contemplated the corruption of man and the four last things, Mikhil Kask broke down. He was fair-haired and sharp-faced, some years older at twenty-four than most of us, and we saw him behind the barrier of a residual European accent. We had been novices little more than a month, and hardly knew one another, least of all Mikhil Kask.

It was the late afternoon. We were scattered. The three storeys of the novices' wing were silent, the only disturbance being the occasional heavy tread along the verandah, or the flushing of a cistern on the first floor. We were idling, by the *piscina*, beside the beehives, along the Rosary Path, at the shrine, past the chook run, on the edges of the oval, when Mikhil Kask screamed. It was verbal, not a mere shriek. "No," he cried. "No, No, No." He was inside the building, somewhere. No one witnessed that first moment. No one saw where the scream came from, or whether it was a denial or a plea. I was not there. I think I heard the far echo of the commotion. No fellow novice took him in hand. Father Kurts, the *Socius*, a reticent, athletic man, came, not running, but rapidly. I have no idea how Mikhil Kask was handled. I never spoke to him and I'm not sure that I ever saw him again. Michael Finnane was questioned by the Master of Novices: Mikhil Kask had claimed, in anguish, "Brother Finnane wouldn't answer me. He wouldn't answer me." Michael Finnane, a gregarious, introverted man, was mystified by the charge. Even if Mikhil Kask, during the strict silence of the Long Retreat, had made some unnoticed overture, why had its rebuff torn out of him that terrible No? I could make no sense of these things. Someone said that as a child, during the war, Mikhil Kask had been in a camp somewhere in Europe. But his breakdown was incidental to my Long Retreat. I locked my vision in and drove forward. I hardly glanced aside as men fell, Michael Liston drowned, Mikhil Kask gone berserk.

In the nature of things novices were inseparable companions, but we exposed to one another very little of the inner man. We saw the tips of histories, but never followed them down. Jim McGettrick, a brother novice and the shape of a wobbly clown, rolled along on his built-up boots. He murmured shyly but laughingly in some rural Leitrim bass. We liked to ask him how he spelt his name. "S, E, A *fada*, M, U, S," he repeated. "For God's sake, Brother McGettrick, talk English," demanded Michael McKernan. Jim McGettrick gave a gentle guffaw and made an indecipherable croaking noise. He was neither skilled nor efficient nor hard-working, but there was love in the teasing of him and in the chuckle with which he received it. He had become a Jesuit as an Australian, not an Irishman. He had the most implacable five o'clock shadow I have ever seen, and he must have been another who came to Australia to die. I had only ever dealt with sophisticated Irishmen before, and Australia was no place for old peasant Ireland to live on. When he was barely forty, Jim McGettrick's heart — which we could have sworn had no strain imposed on it at all — found itself without blood, threshed for an instant, then exploded.

Brian Cash, twenty years older than we were, but grand-fatherly in his grey hair and stoop, came among us from a meandering trail of anonymous occupations. In his husky ear-nestness he leant towards the mere boys he had been elected to live with and told them of his devotional thoughts and was as unworldly as a blind toddler. But one Sunday afternoon we all had a vision of him, in his long grey trousers, sprinting down the right flank of our soccer field on Preston Paddock, more manic and energetic than any player on the field, his hair flying from the thinning forehead, his boots merciless to the wintery stubble, cracking the air with a great attacking yell — "Girls, Girls, Girls". We all stood immobilised, staring upon this worn prophet. Down the hill he streamed, and the desperate savagery of his rush left us stranded. Only when the damp ball hissed from his toe towards the back defence did we recognise the words of his frenzy as a mere rallying cry onwards to the goal. The smouldering grey faded, the hill-spurning strides wound back into the usual shuffle, and Brian Cash slipped over our horizon.

Still God's children came on. Henry van Roosmalen's fea-tures were lost in the several chins and the broken veins of his cheeks, and his English only seemed worth the effort of listening

to because charity suggested it. In his green check jacket he sat
in the furrows of the vegetable garden and swore it was the only
position from which he would prepare the broad bean beds.
There was perversity in the Dutch. Julius Rynders giggled and
sneezed his way through twenty-one poached eggs at second
table breakfast one autumn morning. Mick Dolan, balding at
eighteen, his hands through the slits of his gown beating his
pockets, doubled up in shouted laughter; Peter Pianella, the
confounder of stereotypes, erect and reticent and always just
keeping the smile behind his glasses, a footballer's hands and
shoulders and a cantor's purest gentle tenor; Richard Letters,
the frames of his glasses always lopsided, his favourite, maybe
even his only conversational gambit, the aside.

All casualties. All a one-line slip of paper on the noticeboard.
"Left the noviceship today." All gone before we were allowed to
say goodbye. The first fruits of the fire we were exposed to. The
line of men, tumbling there, closing up here. Yet never so simple
or haphazard as that. Those who fell were those we judged
obviously unfit — the foreign, the extreme, the rough-edged. We
would have chosen them to go. More from our instinct for
orthodoxy than from antipathy, though often enough from that
too. For a man's enemies might well be those of his own household. Charity constrained us, but the laws of natural sympathy
were inexorable. Enclosed as we were we needed less compro-
mising adversaries than our own earthly desires and the workings of Satan. Even in this community of the provisionally
called, we needed to narrow the borders of the elect. Most falls
seemed inevitable. Some we were relieved at, but all we felt
weakened by. The garish and the dissonant were leached away.
The trumpets were quelled. The Master of Novices tried and
found wanting the extravagant assertions of personality.
Generally the younger, still benign shoots, we bent against his
scything. But it was a matter of time. Twenty-three at the start
line and only two to see middle-age as Jesuits. Is there any

interpretation other than loss? Was anyone not a casualty? All the faces scrubbed out. All the faces never registered.

All Things Being Done to Edify

I learnt nothing about evil at Watsonia. We could all be naive or a little sanctimonious or occasional lapsers from observance. Yet neither in myself nor in my colleagues did I face evil in any form — gross or insidious or banal. The possibility didn't occur to me. We were working at the refinements of goodness, not the elimination of evil. My antipathy rose not against vice but against what I saw as wholly virtue. I could not help it. One brother, in his storming of heaven, was a rebuke to me.

As novices we were introduced to the Chapter of Faults. We were invited to offer, in all charity, constructive criticism of each of our brothers. We did it publicly in a controlled, formal setting. Without warning the Master of Novices would put down the Rules or the Constitutions of the Society of Jesus that he was elucidating, and he would announce a Chapter of Faults. He would appear to consider for a moment and then nominate one of us to come out.

When Joe Hackett was called, I was sure there was a rise in tension. Certainly I myself tightened. Joe Hackett went to the front of the Conference Room and knelt beside Father Master with his back to the rest of us, his head inclined at an angle, and his large knuckles clasped across his groin. Father Master ran the side of his finger across under his nose, then stepped back from his lectern, burrowed his hands into his sleeves, and turned his eyes through the window towards the woodpile.

"Brother Finnane," he called.

Michael Finnane gave a start, rolled around on his seat, cleared his throat, folded his arms and put an index finger to the rim of his glasses. His expression was sober. "Brother is very edifying," he began.

It was a second clearing of the throat. It was presumed, universally, that novices were edifying. To use the word without the intensifier made the subject suspect. The word edifying signified the centre of moral excellence. We never spoke of one another as being saintly or holy or good or noble or loving.

Michael Finnane paused. I could not see him, I was in the front row, and we never turned our heads. He repeated the sentence, but this time with an emphasis on the verb, as though he'd become aware of the formulaic nature of the phrase and wanted to repeat it with a more heartfelt, individual application. "Brother *is* very edifying, most edifying." Again he paused. We felt, in fact we hoped, that Michael Finnane, if anyone, could articulate something beyond the inescapable fact of Joe Hackett's edifyingness. Michael Finnane had, after all, a good two years on most of us, he had experienced a world with a different morality, he had some undergraduate legal qualifications that might help him pinpoint and qualify.

In the wider world beyond the Conference Room his opinions were on the loose, and they were both generous and mocking. "The freedom of the Spirit ..." he would chuckle. He clasped his tin mug in both hands and rocked on his heels beside the fire on villa. "We are all given different vocations, all called to different forms of service. The sole end of prayer is contact with God. The means, says Monahan, are all disposable and arbitrary. The position, for example, that you adopt when praying." Michael Finnane guffawed, in anticipation. I laughed too. I could see where he was going. "Kneel, stand, move around, says Monahan, whatever you find best. Joe Hackett, I mean Brother Hackett, has his way. On his kneeler, never leans his chest or even his hands against the front of the desk, and bugger me if he doesn't stretch out his arms in a cross. For an hour, a whole hour, very edifying." Michael Finnane gave a snort of bemusement, but there was some admiration to it. "I sit," he said, and he laughed. He seemed unembarrassed by his own shortcomings as a novice. "Only one trouble at six in the morning. Sitting doesn't lead to prayer. It leads somewhere else." We all laughed. I looked at Michael Finnane. He had a gut, his body was soft. The Society of Jesus, I thought, could give a few lessons in military discipline to the Sydney University Regiment.

"Cripes almighty!" he exploded once as he came out of lunch at twenty past one, his first chance all day to speak freely and in English. Phil Wallbridge was backing away, his body bending in mirth, his finger pointing at Finnane. "And you were in the army! Didn't they teach you?"

We moved towards them, attracted by these raucous preliminaries.

"The *Socius* has been telling me I can't make my bed properly. 'Brother Finnane,' he keeps saying, 'pull it tight, get it straight.'" Michael Finnane stopped as though there were no story, and looked immensely tickled. For all his larrikinism, something dry and withheld persisted in him.

"Ah come on!" Phil Wallbridge yanked his fist round the invisible plot. Then he lost patience, and told it himself. "I had to go down to the dentist yesterday," he began. "Finnane asked me to get him a copy of the *Bulletin*. This morning Kurts called him over as he was coming out of breakfast. 'Brother Finnane,' he says, 'we're going up to your dormitory to fix up this bed-making business, once and for all.' "

Michael Finnane chuckled at his own glorious discomfiture, but said nothing.

Phil Wallbridge made the story his. " 'All right, Brother Finnane,' says Kurts, 'now pull back your bedclothes.' "

Michael Finnane, listening to his own story, gave a sort of twitch.

" 'Right back, Brother Finnane, right off. A new start, Brother Finnane, *ab ovo*.' Finnane goes for the bottom sheet, thinks that if he yanks them all off at once, he might get away with it. 'One at a time, Brother Finnane, they can't get tangled that way.'

Finnane prays that some thief might have forestalled him, he looks at the head of the bed, and flicks the bedclothes as though he's some magician trying to do disappearing tricks. But no luck. Imagine Kurts's face."

We all saw a dry inscrutability, the mouth opening wide and the teeth bared in a stagey, gentle way. Father Kurts lowered his head and drew his splayed hands back across his skull.

" 'Ah Brother Finnane. Paper feet-warmers. You don't need those. We look after you so well.' "

No, Michael Finnane was not edifying. I doubted whether he particularly wanted to be. He had some alternative, occasional code he seemed happy with. So I had hopes for his judgment on Joe Hackett. Joe's piety was enough of a standard and a rebuke to make him a problem for all his fellow novices. I had my own further reason for feeling his presence uncomfortable. Most weekdays we had a Latin class. We worked our way through Cicero's *In Catilinam*, and Joe Hackett's grasp of the more subtle grammatical exceptions of Latin was painfully superior. Yet his manner lacked the brandish of the know-all. He was self-effacing, almost apologetic; no trace of the put-down or of smugness. It was all the more galling; I had no moral come-back against his scholarly triumph. What eased the hurt, and even blurred the discrepancy between us, was the lurching, even chaotic manner of the classes. Father O'Brien took them. He was at an advanced stage of multiple sclerosis. Sometimes he relented and took a wheelchair. Most often his only concession was the black stick, and he teetered the seventy yards to the classroom, his face glistening, his feet never leaving the ground but his knees often bending at right angles as he dragged himself along, spinning out some long-winded jocularity to his beadle. Joe Hackett. And Joe could respond in kind with a laboured common-room pun or a stiff pedantic gloss. Frank O'Brien recapitulated these conversations for the class. "I was saying to *Frater Bidellus*," he began in his lurching quaver as he swayed up from his knees after the prayer, "that our distinction between a beadle and a porter has become, how shall I say, miscegenated ... oh no, that's probably not the ... what shall we call it, the patently apposite descriptive denotation — a philosophical term you'll soon be better acquainted with than I now am." He paused and closed his eyes and his open hand climbed slowly to his head where his taut finger tips shuddered on his forehead. "Now *Frater Bidellus*, or should I say Brother Porter, perhaps we shouldn't spend too long on that. Though our *materia objectiva* is of course words and their meaning and shades of change between languages and eras." He made a twitching, minute, apparently pointless adjustment of his stick's position on the desk.

The lesson went nowhere. I still have no idea what constituted Cicero's case against Catiline. It was an hour and a half most days, for two years, squandered. "Oh ho, d'you see," Frank O'Brien looked up at the clock and remonstrated with himself and us all, "the hour fast approaches when no man can labour any longer. Well yes," he added, "we have, I suppose, considered various matters germane to our central proceedings."

The free flow of his verbal processes never strayed into piety or the struggle of the spiritual life. He said nothing about Calvary. "*Valete, fratres*," he farewelled us. Tense with irritation, and horrified, I watched him take his stick, and drag and quiver his way towards his room.

The hale and the unimpaired had to resort to flamboyant, even melodramatic, gestures to strengthen our faith. Self-humiliation was always affecting. In the refectory, after Grace and before the reading began, we told our faults. At least the novices did so frequently, scholastics sometimes, and priests never. But Father Robert Nash came from Ireland to preach the eight day retreat in the January at the end of our first year of the novitiate. He was in his seventies and renowned as a master of the spiritual life. His publications were many. We had *The Seminarian at His*

Prie-Dieu in our library. In between the very acts of preaching to us Father Nash strode into the refectory, wrapped his gown around his thighs and with practised, surprising agility went to his knees in the middle of the floor. He faced towards the Rector at the far end of the room, and the quadrangle of tables around him on four sides went tight with anticipation. When the Grace was over, and the clatter of people moving their chairs had died away, and while the servers with their hands on their trollies were peering from the kitchen doors in case of this very event delaying their irruption, Father Nash stretched out his arms and unabashed, in a heartfelt voice, cried out, "Reverend fathers and loving brothers, in accordance with holy obedience I tell my fault. In spite of firm resolutions I have most unbecomingly and scandalously lost my temper on two occasions. For which griev-ous fault I ask pardon of God and a penance of my superiors." The Rector nodded at him, almost imperceptibly. Father Nash arched down, kissed the floor, then rose again and went to his place.

The less edifying novices couldn't help their eyes roaming. Michael Sullivan caught Michael Finnane's glance, slid his eyes into the beginning of a roll and leant towards Joe Hackett beside him. "*Panem quaeso, frater,*" he asked. Joe Hackett gave a start, partly because his concentration was disturbed, partly because he was flustered at not having anticipated Michael Sullivan's need for bread.

When Joe Hackett told his own fault, the matter was circum-scribed for him. Father Nash may have been able to target and hammer an uncontrollable temper as his abiding sin, but nov-ices had to choose from a menu not of their own concoction. We were obliged to tell our fault if we were late for morning oblation, the brief prayers in the novices' oratory after we got up, if we returned home late from villa, if we breached major silence, if we spoke on forbidden topics. The common feature of the confessable transgression was that it involved the breach of arbitrary rules, regulations aimed at discipline and good order.

We were novices in the spiritual life. Tendencies to self-flagellation had to be curbed. Why should the more embarrassing or laughable personality defects have to be trotted out, shamefully often perhaps, by young men who were only just starting to ask questions about themselves? Yet the readiness to be exposed — or to expose yourself — was vital, and it was best started with exposure of not too sore a point. Joe Hackett however chafed under the restriction. Very few of the faults were even accessible to him. He had no ability to be late for morning oblation, his night silence was profound. Other people could implicate or deliberately fail him — he favoured, for example, the long villa, and the round trip from Watsonia to Yan Yean or Warrandyte might just not be managed between 10 and 5.30. You saw the pain on the glistening, dangerously overheated freckled face as Joe Hackett, in the lead, came swinging into sight near the fountain at 5.35. Nor could his pain be relieved immediately. He required permission of the Master of Novices to tell his fault.

There was one chance only of going beyond these failures on points of house order. Joe Hackett accused himself of faults against charity. He did not have to be, he was not allowed to be, specific. "I accuse myself of failing in charity," he said.

So, in the Chapter of Faults, Michael Finnane took an oblique approach. "Brother Hackett is most charitable," he repeated. It was a compliment, but it was also a direct contradiction of Joe Hackett himself. What more could Michael Finnane say? The rest of us would not have been capable of taking it further. Certainly Joe Hackett never spoke critically of anyone, there were no barbs anywhere on his tongue, he seemed to live in constant admiration of all his fellows. And in fact actually find them witty and amusing. When he accused himself of being uncharitable, our fancies ran riot at the revelation of a hidden life. We wondered how real these sins against love were, which of ourselves could possibly be the victim of them. Did Joe Hackett sense a pervasive resentment and mockery among his brethren? Did a readily combustible heart smoulder into an anger that was perhaps righteous, but then again perhaps wasn't?

"I wonder sometimes," continued Michael Finnane, "if Brother Hackett isn't a little unbending, not quite relaxed enough, a bit artificial even." We knew what he meant, but he was having trouble with the vocabulary. He had to sound polite, considerate, charitable, and he was trying to apply a code that was natural to him to a personality that was utterly foreign. Father Master nodded slowly in a way that signified understanding of the point and maybe even agreement with it. His expression however stayed far away, and his eyes still focused on the woodheap.

It was six years after I had finished at Watsonia before I revisited it. It was December 1973, and there were four of us, all former residents. The property had been judged superfluous to Jesuit needs and was on the market. For the first time ever I saw the main gates closed, and in fact padlocked. The drive, even in the immediate front of the building where we had clipped and chipped twice a week, was strewn with weeds and runaway grass. We walked around the perimeter of the building; we didn't go inside, and we didn't even knock. A young man, in casual dress, emerged through the boiler room door, swinging a set of keys. When he saw us he diverged from his path towards the garage and we introduced ourselves.

He was a novice. He was one of the last residents of Watsonia. In future any novices would live in Sydney. They were moving out gradually, as they took vows.

"When do you do that?" we asked him.

He gave a date.

"All of you?"

He mentioned an exception.

"He entered late?" we asked.

"No, the same time," he said.

"Ah, he's got a *maturescat*?" said Michael Sullivan.

The novice looked puzzled. The rest of us laughed.

"A *maturescat*," repeated Michael Sullivan with amused impatience. "Don't you have those any more?"

"No, they must have gone," said the novice. He was relaxed in his open ignorance.

We explained the past to him. *Maturescat*. The present subjunctive of the process verb to mature: Let him grow mature. The novice unsure of his vocation, or, more likely, of whose vocation his superiors and the Society were unsure, could be told to prolong his novitiate beyond the two years. He was given a *maturescat*. It would not be for more than a couple of months. If there were still doubt then, he should leave. So maturation, if it were to happen at all, would happen within a matter of weeks. *Maturescat* was a wonderful English noun for us; it was a threat, then a sentence, but also a chance. It was a fabled thing, a matter of part-minatory, part-amusing legend. It was not officially mentioned in any set of rules or processes. The word was never heard from the Master of Novices. It had an unattached, ambivalent life as a term we teased one another with — it might be a disgrace and a stigma but it was also a mark of distinction. The man associated with a *maturescat* belonged to neither the chosen nor the rejected. His progress along the path of perfection was blurred for us.

No one in fact ever got a *maturescat*. The possibility was there — so it was said — in all its complicating potential, but it was never realised.

"Satch," said Michael Sullivan, "Satch Callil got a *maturescat*."

"Did he?" I had no memory of any official word to such an effect. "Were you still there then?"

"He did," insisted Michael. "Old Satch Callil. Temper."

"Really?" It seemed unlikely. None of us had been given a *maturescat*, but we had all left. Whereas warm, muscular, volatile Satch Callil was still a Jesuit. Anyone's money would have to be on his dying a Jesuit.

There are eight hundred men in the ballroom of the Sheraton Wentworth in Sydney. We are all products of Jesuit education. It is 1991 and Ignatius Loyola was born five hundred years ago. We sit at tables of ten. There is a high buzz of conversation and ribaldry. At our table all have been members of the Society of Jesus. Three still are. We are turned half-away from one another towards the stage. The Premier of New South Wales is the keynote speaker. An old boy of Riverview, he refers to the particular and, it would appear, superior virtue, among the religious orders, of the Jesuits. The 800 men applaud.

"What about the Pallotines?" asks someone.

I turn back, laughing. Who has even heard of the Pallotines?

"What about Fr Albert?" adds Michael Sullivan.

We presume Father Albert, the chaplain at Caritas Christi, has died long ago. We have never heard.

"Do the Pallotines still exist?"

No one knows.

It is a night for all the fabled creatures to emerge. Someone long gone from the Society asks after Emmet Costello. Emmet would have been the playboy of the Pacific, he once told us, had he not answered his vocation and entered the Jesuits. However he had never entirely lost touch with that sacrificed lifestyle. He had access to units with harbour views and a Mercedes and the best tailoring and Sydney society. The story to explain these anomalies in the life of a man vowed to Poverty had always been that this was the dispensation of his mother. No one had ever seen her, no one could be sure that she was alive or that she had ever existed. But his own life was the mystery more at hand.

From the far platform some chairman announces there is to be a raffle. "The prize is …" he begins, and Michael Sullivan leans forward and stage-whispers: "to be principal beneficiary of the will of Emmet Costello's mother." His glee is immense.

All of us miss the real, but irrelevant prize.

Michael Sullivan cannot help himself. "Second prize," he says, "is the chaplaincy to Mary Fairfax when Emmet retires."

The Jesuit Provincial speaks of the Society's apostolate. The Jesuit boys are restive. The Provincial tells us that his men should be not so much producing and encouraging the establishment as questioning it. Some attention is being paid him because there are some hisses and boos and cries of protest. Even the members of our own table show they are divided on this issue. There hangs in the air between us a jostle of ideals and betrayals, ambitions and disappointments, credits and compromises. Names are being tossed up, scrutinised.

"What's he ever done?" Michael McKernan is asking Stan Hogan.

I miss the individual's name, but I lean in towards them.

"Well," Stan replies, and it is impossible to tell whether the answer is minimalist or ironic, "he's probably counselled some people."

"Yes, yes," says Michael, "saved souls. That's your bread and butter. But what's he actually done?"

"What's who done?" Michael Sullivan darts in, but there is an outbreak of scattered applause.

I turn and clap.

"Hackett's the one who's done something."

I face the table again.

"Remember the day he left?"

Oddly, I don't.

"Sat down in the ref at lunchtime, shaking. Actually crying. The Mag Nov stands up, sweeps down his serviette, long strides over, leans across the table, flicks his finger. 'Leave,' he says."

I still can't understand why he had to go. An uncharacteristic lack of sympathy from the Novice Master? A stressed personality that I was too young or perpetually unable to discern?

"What's he done?"

"Oh, you've heard."

"No. Was there some rumour he'd become a priest all the same?"

"Oh yes, he found a bishop to take him on for the diocese. Turning into a bit of a heavy there."

"As I would have expected," I say. "He had talent. Of a supremely ecclesiastical … no, that's not fair. Of a religious kind. It was the only place for him. He was sure to do well."

"Flashing?"

"What?"

"Is that what you thought he'd be good at?"

"What?"

"He was in court there a while back. You must've heard about it."

"No, never."

"At the very presbytery door. Trying to exchange cylinders with the paper boy."

"What?"

"He said he liked to feel the air on his body in the early morning. Forgot that's how he was when he opened the door."

"Oh come off it. I don't believe it."

"No. The magistrate didn't either."

I grimace. He is a reproach to us, I think. We cannot let his evident, old-time virtue haunt us. The figures of ancient hagiography, we are now sure, could not be authentic. Men of the world, with or without dog-collars, we know that piety is not just suspect, but a symptom of disorder. You cannot have the Hackett arrray of qualities, and then have the balance, the psychological ease, the ready affectionateness that the certainly good man will display. If we must have such a thing as exemplary virtue, it cannot be the Hackett variety. The imperative oppresses me. So I fear that behind this rumour there is predetermination and wishful thinking. We need never know the truth. We're unlikely ever to want to take the trouble to find out. Joe Hackett is forever as we had suspected. Or perhaps hoped. But forever that.

The taxis slide from their queue in Elizabeth Street and in under the portico of the Sheraton. We jostle and separate, sweaty and pale under the harsh light.

"Christ, I don't want to go home yet," I hear someone say. "Where should we go on to?"

Making Ourselves Eunuchs

Matthew, 19.12

We were not to touch one another. As we were never to touch anyone.

When Mary turned and saw Christ by his tomb she thought it was the gardener, and she asked where the body had gone. Christ called to her. "Mary," he said. The single word, the lip-parting release of her name, could only have been tender. It was her own name, kindling all her nerve ends in the warmth of its evocation, that revealed him to her. It was the voice, naming her, and issuing from that body, that restored him to her. "Rabbini," she answered him, and her impulsive hands went out in delight to the one that had been lost and was now found. Yet she was held back. Not by his firm grip, nor even by an extended arm, but by his voice. "Do not touch me," he said. It was a singular moment in the record of his life. Amidst all the exhortation and storytelling, there juts this moment of raw, personal defensiveness. He might tell his parents that he must be about his Father's business, but he returns home with them. He might tell his mother that the wine running out is no business of his, but he transforms the water. He might ask Peter if he loves him, but the moment is a public ritual. But in the garden, when Mary falls towards his rediscovered body, he cries out in sudden prohibition, and she comes no closer. "Do not touch me," he says, "for I am not yet ascended to the Father, to your Father and to my Father." It is the most opaque thing he ever said.

We knew the prohibition simply as the *ne tangas* rule. It was often invoked, in a laughing manner. Michael Sullivan accused Stan Hogan of an uncharitable slur against one of his brothers. Stan Hogan closed his fists, hunched down, and shaped up. Michael Sullivan withdrew, laughing and calling loudly, "*Ne tangas*, brother, *ne tangas*". Michael Sullivan liked to quote the fullness of the rule. "Do not touch, *ne etiam in ioco*." Not even in fun. The rule might have been laughed at, but it was not broken. Novices and scholastics did not put their arms around one another's shoulders, did not slap on the back. They did not wrestle, nor lay a hand on another's arm in encouragement or affection. Only one exception was made. At the end of the novitiate, those two years of probation, when we took vows as scholastics, we were released from soccer, cosmopolitan and body-contact free, and told to play the local game. The collision of the joint mark, the hip or shoulder or elbow engaging in the tussle for the loose ball, these gestures of antagonism were allowed. At its most charged and active the body could position itself to ward off or nullify the other body. But when the final whistle sounded, we stamped and crunched our way back along the cinder path, under the dark cypresses, a snorting, steaming body of single men, to our cubicles.

I worked out the logic of the affective life in class. In black gowns, often faded or patched or grubby, over our old secular clothes, we crammed the long tables in the Conference Room. The Master of Novices worked through the guiding principles of our calling. I knew about the centrality of love. But the emotional life, instinctual and spontaneous love — as opposed to charity, the central duty of the Christian vocation — I knew nothing of that. I was there to learn. The Master of Novices dictated to us, and then took questions.

"If love of a spouse, Father," I asked him, "detracts from the love we give to God, why doesn't the love of another person as a friend do so too?"

Father Master saw the problem. He did not dismiss my question. He found no fault with my logic. The premiss was given. Our celibacy was founded on it. And given the premiss the consequent did seem to follow. Yet the practice of the Church was otherwise; I knew that myself. Ignatius had loved Francis Xavier, Francis de Sales had loved Jeanne-Françoise de Chantal. Father Master said he would have to think about it further.

I pressed the point. "As we know, marriage is a good thing, but celibacy is a more perfect following of Christ?"

Father Master nodded.

"Yet celibacy, the more perfect way, is a vocation, to which only some are called."

"Yes ..."

"Well why not the same with friendship? It too is the normal way, but there is a higher vocation to which a chosen few are called. To be without friends. 'Let him take it who can' as Christ says about celibacy."

"I see your point. I see your point." Father Master nodded his head slowly.

I saw no alternative. If I had given up everything to follow the more perfect way, there was no point now in not electing to follow that more perfect way. Why aspire to sanctity and then so knowingly settle for second best?

After two years we vowed ourselves to poverty, to obedience, and to chastity. We were scholastics, no longer novices. We were free now to choose our own company. Thursday was still villa day, but there were no longer any formal requirements.

I left my room and came down for morning tea.

"Are you going on villa?" asked Simon Campion.

"I'm not sure," I said, "I haven't decided." I poured my tea, and went over to the billiard table to idle through the spread-out *Age*.

Paul Schulze came and stood opposite. He leant across the

cushions and said in a low voice. "Gerry, will you come on villa with me?" Paul Schulze was a coadjutor brother. He had been a sheet-metal worker.

"Why not, Brother Schulze?" I said.

"It's a few months since we've been out together," he persisted. "I'll get things ready."

"Thanks, Brother Schulze," I said. "I'll see you down here. Say, half past eleven."

"What about eleven o'clock?"

"I've got too much to do. Half past will give us plenty of time."

I went away to wash my cup and saucer. Simon came into the sink room through the verandah door. "Have you decided yet?" he said.

"I've arranged with Brother Schulze. Would you like to come?"

He stood still an instant, and, with my back to him, I ran the cold tap over my crockery. "I might," he said, as I reached for the tea towel and was careful not to look at his face. Abruptly he turned through the door and clattered up the stairs. "No, I won't," he called, and the forced tone was of reluctant refusal on a trivial matter. The rough, hasty stamp of his footsteps faded.

Beside us the rocky, tussocked slope fell away steeply to the Plenty. We sat where the winter sun caught the lumpy luxuriant grass. The larger sticks in the fire had reached their maximum glow. The billy was in place. The smoke lurched and drifted between us without favour. I watched the brown blush spread across the slice of bread at the end of my wire.

"Did you go on picnics with your family, Gerry, when you were in *mundo*?" Paul Schulze asked me.

I was still a curious animal to him. He had no experience of families. He had known only an orphanage.

"Oh yes, but they were different." I reversed the slice of

bread. "Did you ever go home and stay with a family, Brother Schulze?" I asked. "At Christmas, say?"

"Ohh no," he said. He raised his eyebrows and blinked, and his tongue played briefly with a dental plate. "Well, as a matter of fact, I nearly did, once."

"Why, what happened?"

"Well, I was supposed to go. So Sister said. But I didn't."

I felt he would have left it at that. I prised the bread from the wire and handed it around the fire to him. He gripped the slice in the bowl of his hand, and prodded and kneaded the butter across it. I thought to myself, I should have swapped the food preparation roles.

"Why, what happened?" I repeated.

"Oh well, nothing much really. I thought I was going to go, but I didn't." He held the bread on his outstretched hand. "Vegemite or jam, Gerry?"

I pointed to the Vegemite. "Thanks." I pinned another slice of bread to my wire. "Why didn't you go?"

He handed me his heavily tanned work. "I don't know," he said. "I couldn't tell you."

I twisted the question into him. "What exactly happened? I'm interested." I kept my face averted from him and I stared into the unchangeable orange of the coals.

Sister told Paul he was going to stay with a family for Christmas. Most of the other children who had been chosen had already gone. Sister helped him pack his bag, gave him a glass of milk, and put him on a chair on the low verandah at four o'clock to wait for his family. He leant forward, his fingers under his knees, and swung his legs. He had never been to a family before, and Sister hadn't told him anything about this one. Only to be good and to have a happy and holy Christmas and to remember Jesus. For Paul and all the children from the Home had a special place in the Holy Family. This other family wouldn't have a chapel in their home. What would he do, he wondered, when he got up? Would the parents clap their hands and turn on the lights? Would they just appear? Did you see where the parents lived, in a family? Paul kicked his legs so that he could see his toes above the pruned rose bushes just beyond the verandah. He jerked higher and higher so that he soared above the poppies along the border of the flower bed. The yellow, the pink, and the orange bursts were no match for his swings. Higher and longer he swung till the flowers drooped and shrank in on themselves and the heat began to fade out from the day.

"Gracious me," said Sister when she came through the front door. "You still here, Paul?"

"Yes, Sister."

"Haven't they come?"

"No, Sister."

"Well I don't think they'll be coming now. It's nearly seven o'clock, past dinner time. You'd better come back inside and have something to eat."

"Yes, Sister."

"Bring your bag with you. Take it up to your locker, and then come downstairs. We'll fix something up for you."

At the end of my fork the bread flamed and blackened. "Oops, I'll have to try again. Would you like it well or lightly done, Brother Schulze?"

"Paul, please Gerry. We're not novices any longer."

"Very good," I said.

As scholastics we emerged in a line from dinner, and, on the portico, formed pairs strictly according to that line. The custom was that we remained in those pairs for one vigorous circuit of the property. After that we were free to mingle, talk, play pool, have coffee, give one another haircuts. On Monday nights I went up into the Tower. The Tower rose from the centre of the build-ing, a square castellated block, barely higher than it was wide.

On each exterior surface was a large circle in cement relief, with four arms radiating from it at right angles. The design stood against the sky in the shape of a giant monstrance. In the circle that faced towards the east was a large porthole window.

The Tower was our Bindery. The porthole window was high and behind a workbench and we rarely looked through it. Most scholastics spent three-quarters of an hour there one evening a week. Surrounded by archival stacks of *Austral Light* and *The Advocate*, we stripped off our gowns and put on dark navy aprons and moved in among the stanley knives and guillotines and pots of glue and sheets of plain pressed cardboard and bolts of garish, coarse-stitched cloth. We were to rebind paperbacks. The library had eighteenth century volumes of philosophy and theology whose covers were detached and whose leaves were falling out and being lost, but we never touched these books. We slit the covers from *Animals Without Backbone*, a Pelican book that had been bought in multiples so that we could get a zoological underpinning for the Psychology we were to do. We cut out boards for a shelf of F. C. Copleston's *Aquinas*. We threw away the illustrated, laminated wrap-arounds that were beginning to replace the unadorned covers of the earlier Penguins. We did so although these books would never be handled or read so much that their original bindings would become loose and broken-backed. We just took them from the shelves in the library and carried them to the bindery and went to work on them. I ruined some with bindings so tight they could no longer be opened, and others with boards so misshapen and overlapping that they would not stand balanced on the shelves, and others again with violent-coloured cloth or protuberant lumps of glue or crude lettering on the spine, so that no one would ever willingly handle them. Others again defeated me, defeated other crafts-men, and the bindery was littered with flayed books whose tormentors had given up on them or left the house, thought-lessly. In time I eased back from the workbench, and observed and talked and stood around. Then I retreated from the Tower altogether.

Only one scholastic taught himself to bind with any proficiency. Marciano Baptista, who had come from Macau for his Philosophy, did in fact bind with flair. On my twenty-first birthday, when I had been at Watsonia for three years, Marciano brought me a present. He came to my cubicle and handed me something in a brown paper bag. He stood and waited, a sinuous splayed pose to his limbs, his fingers long and restless. I unwrapped a black slipcase, with twin half-circular indentations cut out where the thumb and forefinger could grasp the spine of the protected book. It was a Fontana paperback, a newly published translation of the Psalms. Marciano had left intact the illustrated cover with its bas relief of a blind man playing an eight-stringed harp. But he had glued to the spine a new binding, a piece of white, greying hide, cut so that it just overlapped, with precise evenness, the edges of the book. These were vaulted with another small flap that clipped tight to a clasp on the back cover. Finally Marciano had inserted a marker ribbon of scarlet silk and laid on, top and bottom, headbands of alternating red and pale lemon.

The neat opulence of it flooded me. I could not remember a gift ever bringing me such pleasure. Unexpected, beautiful, and I would use it. I wanted to use it. Day after day.

Marciano's fingers bounced across his chin. He clicked from his right foot to his left and back again. I shook my head and my shoulders rose slightly and then collapsed again. Underneath the admiration and gratitude I felt, there shivered an uneasiness. I wasn't sure about presents to one another. I was not quite happy with either the gesture or the implication of ownership that Marciano's gift involved. Yet the sight and the handling and the prospect of use of this book lapped at me. "It's terrific," I said. "You've done a marvellous job."

Marciano shrugged, and smiled. He went out without another word, asking for nothing more.

I got a pencil and in a small, faint script I wrote inside the book: *ad usum* G. Windsor S.J. Loyola. Watsonia.

Years later, in middle-age, I try to rethink all this as normal patterns of human friendship. I am haunted by a dream of an incident that took place not at Watsonia, but at the diocesan seminary at Werribee where we went as scholastics in the summer. I tackle Michael McKernan.

"One night," I put it to him, "Christmas of '67, when we were on holidays at Werribee, we had a row on the front lawn there. In front of the Chirnside mansion. What was the argument about?"

He looks hard at me. "Oh you were a right bastard at that time."

I can't tell whether he remembers the occasion or not.

"So bloody censorious," he says. "I'd probably had a drink or something."

"It was sunbaking actually. That's what you were doing. In direct contravention of the letter of Father General on the subject to the whole Society."

"Exactly! I ask you!"

Together we laugh.

"Still," I say, "given that we were Jesuits ... what sort of attitude would you have liked from me? It's not as if I was delating you."

"Come on. You can wear your disapproval in technicolour."

"What were we arguing about?" I repeat. I can see us in the moonlight, and feel my own heels digging into the crisp summer lawn. "I resented, no ... I objected to, the hold you had on various people."

"You were extraordinarily intolerant. There was only one

way of doing things, one correct philosophy. I had a more relaxed, eclectic outlook."

"I'd say people were actually dependent on you."

"Poor lads."

"We both had our followings, I know that."

"Power. It was all about power of course."

"I've never been interested in power."

"Well you mightn't be very good at going about getting it, but you sure did resent other people having it."

He says this in an overblown expostulatory way, so that it is impossible to take offence.

"It was more complicated than that," I say. "You were a very attractive personality, and it's not surprising that you drew people to you."

"Not surprising at all."

"I'd say I felt that attraction too. But I wasn't going to be anybody's stringer. Anything that smacked of emotional dependence was humiliating. I despised others for it. I half admitted to myself that you were the most attractive personality there but I wasn't going to be drawn to you. Still, I was aware of your pull. We had to move on separate tracks. But we stayed parallel. I could always see you out of the corner of my eye."

"Mmm," he says.

We take it no further. But I remember the elation in that bitter stand-off. The content seems irrecoverable. Light barely leaked from behind the shutters in the few priests' rooms in the mansion, Major Silence was in force throughout the premises. We danced around one another on the lawn, in the lee of the first bed of canna lilies. I was keyed-up on accusation, wincing at the sting of counter-charge, trembling with indignation and pleasure, conscious that at last we were meeting without restraint or any of the glancing politesse of courtesy and religious decorum. The intensity of the contact was searing.

In 1993, on Children's Day, the last day of the Royal Easter Show, in the early afternoon, I went to the Commemorative Pavilion. It is the time the District Produce displays are dismantled and the items sold off. I was after jam and chutney and pickles, but all they were releasing were whole pumpkins and marrows and apples and other long-lasting, sturdy produce. So I walked on past the massive crumbling mosaics of fruit and vegetables towards the exit. In the far corner I noticed display cases devoted to honey. I thought I might still be lucky. Behind the glass hung trays of honeycomb, invisibly supported. On stands, at different levels, stood the honey jars. I saw the even viscosity of the liquid, its unclouded purity, the pale modesty of its appeal. The distinctive broad ribbons of the Royal Agricultural Society were draped among the jars and the award certificates. I went down on my haunches to look. I read on one, and then on another, and then, it seemed, on all of them that the winning exhibitor was Canisius College, Pymble. Who was this, I wondered, who was doing such things for the Society of Jesus? And I wished to sample the honey.

I creaked up on my stiff legs and looked around. There was a booth nearby and it was attended. I walked over and began to speak to the grey-bearded man.

"Is the prize-winning honey for sale?" I looked about on the shelves and the counter. "I'd actually like one of the Canisius College varieties. It doesn't matter which."

The man and I looked at one another.

"Paul," I said.

"Gerry," he said.

"So it's you, all this honey."

"Yes. Yes."

"It's marvellous. Congratulations. I'd love to try some."

He put his right foot back, and held up his left hand, and as he strained for a sentence the unformed breath popped in his throat. "I haven't got any," he said.

"To buy, I mean."

"No," he said. "It isn't for sale." The creases rolled up his high forehead and his head bobbed. "I need it, for the Hawkesbury Show."

"I'd love to try some," I repeated.

"You can call in some time, Gerry," he said. He rubbed his knuckles together and blinked. It was impossible to tell what he was thinking. "Come to the front door and ask for me," he said.

Now I lie beside my son.

"Dad," he says, "you can't really have a best friend."

"How do you mean? Why not?"

"Umm," he starts and repeats several times. "Umm … like first best and second best and third best … Like Joel said I was his best friend. But Niki …"

I wait. "I don't quite get what you mean." Across the pillow I feel the muscles tightening down his temples.

"Well, best …" he begins. He hesitates. His head flickers in dismissal. "It doesn't matter."

Dissatisfaction itches me. I try to isolate the different possibilities of meaning and hold them in focus.

"Dad," he says.

"Yes."

"Tickle me."

"Oh," I say. "Sure." I hold my breath, go stock still, pump up the tension. Then I turn on my side, in slow menace, and bring my face close down over his. My right hand hovers around his neck and his armpits. My left hand reconnoitres up and down the rest of his body.

"No, Dad, no, Dad," he laughs, shuddering and warding off the feints I make. "Wait, wait."

"You told me to. I do what I'm told." My fingers dance just below his collarbone. His palm flutters against them.

"Stop, stop, you can only use one hand."

"What! Says who?" But my fingers die. His grip closes over them. His eyes widen, he draws in his breath.

"Righto then," I warn. The pincer snaps on his thigh.

"Hey, hey," he bucks, rolling away to the right, threshing with his head and shoulders.

Thumb and forefinger loosen and compress. The flesh is so taut, so smooth.

"Ah, ah, ah," he gasps.

I release and reapply the pressure. "Is it tickling yet?" I call. I watch his face. I listen hard to the howls.

"Stop, stop," he shouts.

I ease momentarily, then tighten the pressure again.

"Hey Dad, hey Dad," he yells. "I haven't said all the rules yet!"

I Applied My Heart to Wisdom

Ecclesiastes 7.25

For three years after I finished my novitiate I studied Philosophy. It gave me pets. Creatures I observed and nourished and grew fond of. I could not help it. The pared abstractions of the wise turned into scampering animalculi.

David Buckingham, the youngest of us, started it all. After our two years as novices we took vows as true Jesuits, and in gleaming, unspotted clericals we advanced in ragged line across the quadrangle lawn to the other, northern, side of the house. We turned our backs on our juniors, and the philosophers stepped off their own verandah and advanced to meet us. David Buckingham, tight-shouldered, plunged ahead, his stiff hand pumping down as he took congratulations. He bounded on in front into Philosophy. We started with Minor Logic, and within weeks, we decided, David Buckingham was in thrall to the Singular Proposition. I was unsure of the Singular Proposition; it had something to do with statements about "the Author of Waverley". The very arcaneness of Sir Walter Scott and the double distancing of the circumlocution, made the Singular Proposition remote and exotic. But David Buckingham seemed attached to it.

He embraced it as the first secular, non-Jesuit acquaintance he'd made in two years. I never knew what he did with it. I didn't trust it myself, I didn't know how to handle it, I kept my distance. Yet David Buckingham domesticated it. He was a prodigious walker, and I imagined he took the Singular Proposition out with him. David's single-minded, relentless boots pushed away at the ground, and beside them the Singular Proposition, rich in extraordinary abilities as his name suggested, hopped and bounced, never following the same trajectory twice, a sunny, tireless, scampering child. He was so elastic that he could spring up and shoot the breeze with David, mouth to mouth, always capable of handling any knotty one that furrowed David's brow, then subsiding again and adapting to the long, punishing rigour of the boots. They were inseparable friends, and we teased David about the attachment.

In time he didn't speak so often about the Singular Proposition, and other attachments came into his life. He took up with Marxism and I think the Singular Proposition might have been left in the lumber room of first loves. Yet his maturer affections seemed to me vast, lumpy grotesqueries, and I could never imagine the boyish familiarity with them that he had enjoyed with the Singular Proposition.

For all my inability to share his choice, his example was a potent one. I was looking out for a creature of my own.

When, as a schoolboy, I had entered the front parlour at Riverview — which was so rare that I could recall no specific occasion for it and wondered if I ever went there at all — there were two objects that engrossed me. One was a dim painting, in a craggy, corrugated gold frame. It was high and smoky, and in it a woman held up by the hair and displayed direct to the viewer the severed head of a bearded man. The Death of John the Baptist. I didn't understand its connection with the school. He was not the patron. He had no specific significance. I found the message hard to get. The dead eyes were shut, the whole face blank of the kind of significance I expected — neither serenity nor triumph. Hairy and tousled should not have been the final state of Christ's Precursor. Salome was odd too. She did not look like a dancer. She wore a voluminous dress of deep purple, its pendulous sleeve hanging as low and heavy as the Baptist's head. Her gaze was calm rather than shameless.

On the other side of the room, on a massive sideboard, under a semi-oval glass cover on a stand, was a faded pink skull cap.

A typed slip of paper inside the glass said that the cap was Cardinal Newman's. I didn't know what to make of this. I thought it most unlikely that such an object should be sitting on a cakestand in the parlour at Riverview. Cardinal Newman had never had any connection with the place. Yet I knew that such a cap would have a power. My grandmother had a first cousin a bishop, and she said that if you touched a bishop's skull cap, you'd never suffer from headaches; the bishop had said he was never without them. In spite of all that, when I looked at the Riverview cap and although it sat deflated and concave and puckered around the edges, I did feel a little awed. It wasn't impossible that it was genuine, and, if so, it was the first true relic I had seen.

These images of the past intrigued me. I hardly knew why. I didn't understand their presence here at Riverview. Much less why they should mean anything to me. Later on I was told Newman's headgear was a *zucchetta*, not a skull cap. I was also told that the bloody couple across the room were not Salome and John the Baptist, but Judith and Holofernes. The new designations fitted the facts better. It made more sense of things. Yet as to why these relics appealed to me, I was really no wiser.

The study of Greek and Latin was the core of a Jesuit education. When I was a schoolboy at Riverview, two priests taught me Classics. Between the arches of the quadrangle there were garden seats, painted white, and facing inward. Father Austin Ryan sat there; and he talked with anyone who might join him. Father Ryan hung his head, and there were large moles on his face, and a tic to his chin which pulsed in time with a grunt, an invitation to assent that followed all his statements. His index finger jerked between an itchy probe under his collar and a rapid scratch in the wiry grey hedge of his hair. He was always puzzled and solicitous. His nerves came to the surface and rubbed raw as he worried over what he taught his pupils.

Father Charles Fraser took over the Classics from him. Sharp and nasal and reactive in his speech, Father Fraser set rabbit traps around the property and played squash with boys and loved his roses.

"I think," he said to me, "that the *Apology* is the third greatest book ever written. And Socrates the second greatest man, mere man, that ever lived."

I couldn't resist the obvious questions.

"Saint Paul," he said, "but otherwise I put Socrates ahead of all the saints."

This seemed wondrous to me.

"Mind you, Father Ryan would tell you differently."

"Would he?"

"Oh he thinks Socrates a most terrible creature."

I couldn't understand that. Socrates was a martyr, a man who wouldn't apostatise.

"It's all those questions. He had no respect for the traditions and forms of things. Of a civilised people. No awareness of the destruction he was causing. No thought of where he might end up."

Father Fraser went on at length, but he seemed merely to be summarising Father Ryan. I couldn't see any harm done. We had read through the *Apology* so many times, Father Fraser and I, that I almost knew it by heart. Socrates was always polite and reasonable.

"Father Ryan has his own views about the Greeks though," added Father Fraser. "Thinks the *Iliad* is a lot of rubbish. Just glorified cowboys and Indians."

I was sure Father Ryan was wrong. The *Iliad* was the greatest poem ever written. Still, I saw what he meant and I wasn't quite sure how you distinguished the *Iliad* from a western.

When I went to Watsonia, Father Fraser presented me with a copy of Thomas à Kempis' *Imitation of Christ*. For Father Fraser this was the second greatest book ever written. He inscribed it to me with a line from the *Iliad*, in Greek, an exhortation by "the good Diomedes" to Achilles: "Always be the bravest [or the best] and go beyond others, and never shame the line of your fathers." I was glad that as novices we did not pick up one another's books and that very few of my fellows could read Greek. Such a value system seemed impossible to square with any Jesuit personality evolving in me.

I turned, as long as I was a novice, to *pius Aeneas*. When I took vows and was primarily a student again, and was receiving a second Jesuit education, the ghost of Achilles clashed his arms together a second time. "Read Newman's *University Sermons on Faith and Reason*," said the reticent Father Daly, warming us up for his classes on Epistemology.

I began at the beginning. Newman called his opening sermon, preached when he was only twenty-five, "The Philosophical Temper, First Enjoined by the Gospel". I could hardly get past the beauty of the title — the lovely ancient words, the even largeness of the claim, the perfect unity of life envisaged. I read on into Newman and never stopped. I believed in the enterprise of this life, I warmed to the man engaged in it. "They shall know the difference now that I am back again," trumpeted the sulky, blood-lusting Achilles returning to the fight after the death of his cousin Patroclus. "They shall know the difference now that I am back again, " promised the self-conscious, wry young clergyman reaching Oxford from Sicily, ready to combat what his friend John Keble had just called "national apostasy". I liked that. This was the true drama, and in the right heroic terms. I liked the incarnate, grappling God that Newman set his bearing for. *Ex umbris et imaginibus in veritatem*, Newman wanted for his epitaph. From shadows and reflections into truth. Trying to palpate this God, that's what we should be doing, storming through the abstractions in as bodily a way as we could. Aquinas in the same quandary; overwhelmed by the late stroke of mystical vision, shrugging off a life's work in describing his God: "it is as straw".

Still, straw would do for a start — the tawny, fibrous, brittle leftover, the basic stuff of every crib, the material to be spun into gold. Shavings of the sacred. I would have to ask and feel my way to it.

Once we were scholastics there began the centrifugal drift from the tight Jesuit model of the novitiate. We now lived in wooden cubicles, the dividing walls seven feet high, so that we heard but did not see one another. In the long corridor outside we knew one another's comings and goings only by the pattern of footsteps. A year later we were assigned rooms, in the corners of the building, with one window each on to the grounds. We had a private life to begin, a room to make our own. Only once a day was that privacy waived. Some time between six and seven in the morning — it was never wholly predictable — the beadle opened the door of the room without knocking and looked to see that we were, at least outwardly, at prayer. Otherwise the room was ours, and individuals emerged. The two-year stalling of personalities was over. In each room there was a spurt of growth, or growths. Phil Wallbridge vaulted into the tractor seat and ranged the property, the low clanking gangs rolling and wheeling behind him, racing ahead of the dry wave of cut grass. Vince Hurley covered himself in grey cotton and a gauze net and chortled and bustled the bees into releasing drum after drum of honey. Jim Kilbride built himself a machine for reading in bed. He had been a farmer and he was now a philosopher. He could lie supine, his hands any way he wished, his book above him face down on a spotless plate of thin glass set in a wooden frame, supported by swivelling arms and metal-toed legs. He still had to turn the pages manually, so he preferred slower-moving, ruminative books when he was in bed.

Stan Hogan filled his room with books. It was known as the extra library in the house. Downstairs, in our general library, there was a small shelf of books, *Eyeless in Gaza*, *The Essential James Joyce* … marked NSL, *Ne Sine Licentia*. They could only be borrowed with permission, but permission was given whenever it was asked. Now, invisibly, apparently overnight, the corpus of modern and modernist literature appeared in Stan Hogan's room. Faulkner and Fitzgerald and Steinbeck and Beckett and Genet and Pinter and Osborne. I was interested, but never asked to borrow. It was a point of conscience; I did not have permission for these books.

We were free to invite others into our room, but I did not actively do so. I kept my room uncluttered and undecorated. I went running, I dug vegetable beds for Lem, but no activity was a passion. I waited behind my desk, facing the door, but always with a book in front of me. I was moving into Bernard Lonergan's *Insight: A Study of Human Understanding*, the 785 pages of it. It was a responsible act of faith; the book was by a Jesuit, it had only been published eight years before, it set itself "to augment and perfect the old with the new", a phrase and a program of Pope Leo XIII and the one exigent mind that taught us had found in it, unostentatiously but securely, his credo. I set it on my lectern, and the black, white, grey, and scarlet cover began to define my intellectual landscape. Centred right were red ink strokes done with a brush, sharp lines and angles relaxing just once or twice into sinuous rolls. I had been looking at this abstract for three months when I realised in a flash that it was eyes and wrinkled brows and the thinker's traditional chin rest of a hand. After that I closed my eyes and shifted focus and moved angles, but the face would not leave me. I could find no other way of interpreting those dashes and squiggles. I had put them together again in a way the artist had done originally. Intellect, I read, is capable of creating, and of itself turning into, everything. The mind is, in a sense, everything. The understanding is infinitely protean, rolling away into costume changes, into the magician's tugs that spill cloth, ribbons, flowers, into the televisual heave and pulse of successive graphics. There is one centre of consciousness becoming all these things. And seeking endlessly the flashing moments that will give it a new shape, a new presence. That old human mind, powered by a restless, detached spirit of inquiry that forever wants to understand. Call it wonder, the source of all wisdom.

The simple power of this oddly practical, immediately usable, vision quivered there in the dark, shadowed room. I held the insight and I couldn't credit it. I tried to hold it steady and take a firm grasp. Everything given its meaning by the same irrepressible transformer. Hence everything so alike. The harmonious unity of it all. Each meaning existing because a mind had put it together and released it from undifferentiated chaos. I went back to the small black marks on the 785 white pages and my mind moved among them juggling and grouping, and then plucking up a new shrieking idea that I held in the air, marvelling and nervous, till my excitement was gathered in, and I moved on, and the idea slipped away, to reemerge when I sought it.

This was not Latin textbook stuff. This was what I could do. This was what I caught myself doing. I went round the corner of my room, just past the showers, into the classroom, and I heard a confident, unprepared burble about Ethics or a detached, alienated display of Metaphysical Psychology. Principles and tags and maxims and terms bobbed past. None of them seemed to possess or be possessed of any urgency. They floated on, in a rolling, half exposed way, doing the circuit of some river of tradition where every seminarian, as far back and as far forward as imagination reached, paddled fitfully and then stepped out. The mind was forever being dipped in the magical stockpot of the Church's Styx.

I was paddling there too. It was a piece of flotsam that snagged itself against me. *Intellectus agens*, said the washed-out label. I just liked the name. It seemed incidental and without connections, another gratuitous ingredient of this eternal brew. I wondered how it had got there, if there'd ever been any sense in its invention. I liked the name. I couldn't ignore the *intellectus agens*. I went and knocked on Tom Daly's door. Tom Daly had been an engineer before he became a Jesuit. He sat at his desk, always in his full clericals and gown, hunched by the window cramped against the corner of the building. There was no adornment to his room at all. The colour scheme was given by his chair and narrow desk and the neat stacks of bulging brown manilla folders. His Epistemology course was an activities program, not a doctrine, to make us reflect on our cognitional activities, distinguish the structure of them, and be the better thinkers for that self awareness. And be the better men, nearer to God. For Christ was the full expression of the mind of the Father. That was a slog, reaching into the mind of God. Or into our own minds. Tom Daly was uncompromising about that. No matter the question asked him, he would avoid saying Yes.

I asked him if he were busy. He never said he was, but nor did he smile or relax or bother with preliminary small-talk. He gestured to his vinyl armchair.

"The *intellectus agens*," I said. "I've never heard of it before. Where does it fit in?"

Tom Daly knew I was talking about another lecturer's offering. He crossed his legs. The light flashed on his glasses. "Ahhh," he gutturalled, but there was a slight question at the end of it. I was to go on.

"It seems a superfluity."

"It could, it could."

"Well, I haven't got an *intellectus agens*."

"Ah, haven't you." Tom Daly made it sound like a statement, a realisation of his own.

"But it's in the textbooks." I tried to be progressively logical, and not sound frustrated.

Tom Daly waited.

"It sounds as though it slipped in there once — heavens knows how — and now they're just reproducing it."

"Ah. How's that?"

Tom Daly made me move carefully. It wasn't intimidation. Not quite. There was no menace, no threat of a pounce. It was the absence of exuberance, everything being tested in the back of the throat, and then perhaps being allowed to pass, never chewed and swallowed with avidity.

"Well," I speculated, "someone did have some sort of an insight once, and labelled the result the *intellectus agens*. No one's had the insight since, but they've all stuck with the term. A meaningless term."

"That happens."

"So I have to have the insight too, to make any sense of it?"

"The insight might be that there is no sense."

"Well … yes." I was stumped, couldn't see a way to move.

Tom Daly waited, patient for my next question. His mouth was half open, his eyebrows twitching against the frames of his glasses. One hand held the edge of his desk, set to pull him back to work as soon as I made to leave.

I started again. "It's not doing anything. Nothing I can identify. It just seems to be spoken of as hanging around all the time. But it's not given any function, just spoken of as some evolutionary dead-end. A sort of appendix."

Tom Daly shifted on his chair and wrapped his gown more tightly around his knees. "More a preliminary." He couldn't resist the metaphorical play.

I was thrown. Perhaps jolted. This was too like a lead. "A preliminary?" I repeated.

"It might make more sense." Tom Daly retreated, sounded doubtful, or at least exploratory.

Still, I had grasped the clue. "Ah, more than a preliminary," I said. "More a *sine qua non*."

Tom Daly showed no sign of liking the Latin.

"Our natural desire to know?" I said.

"Read Aristotle's *De Anima*," said Tom Daly.

I hardly heard him. "The unavoidable itch to know," I said.

The westering sun edged in and caught Tom Daly from behind. I lost his features. His glasses sparkled and his soft brown hair crackled. The light swelled and advanced so that he was a fuzzy silhouette. I got up and let it push me through the door. The *intellectus agens*, he'd do me for a pet. I liked the old name, and if I was going to cut out one companion from the flotsam of three years' philosophy, this timeless urge couldn't be bettered. He was the one to feed and make a companion of. I liked the crisp, steely feel of him. My *intellectus agens*.

At the end of our five years at Watsonia we took an exam known as the *De Una*. Translated immediately and most literally it was an exam "on one matter" or "on the one thing". There was an echo of an understood word, in the Latin, *re*, and beyond that the somehow even stronger echo of the phrase "the one thing necessary". That one thing was the salvation of one's soul. Judged by the eye of heaven nothing else mattered.

Yet in fact *De Una* was not short for *De Una Re*. *Una* was an abbreviation for *Universa*. It was not one thing, but everything. It was, most fully and precisely, *De Universa Philosophia*. We took an exam in The Whole of Philosophy, or perhaps The Universal Philosophy. By custom everyone passed.

The Drama in Our Lives

In *Double Feature*, the third volume of his autobiography, the actor Terence Stamp makes no mention of his visit to Loyola College, Watsonia, in the early summer of 1965. Yet his appearance there was memorable.

When I was seventeen and at school I had fallen on my sword, as Brutus, in the debacle of Philippi, and then given up (as I was about to give up all else) my life on the stage. The move had an appropriateness to it. The call to the Christian and, above all, to those invited to the more perfect following of Christ was to put off all vain posturings, all empty and idle fantasies and imaginings.

The Christian vocation demanded of each soul that it cast aside all disguise and come out naked into the presence of God. It told me that the Lord himself was my illumination. It reminded me that this appearance was brief, but that it was watched by a vast cloud of witnesses. It encouraged me by emphasising that I was little less than the angels, but then it warned me that I was a worm and no man.

The tenor of this drama was plain and uncompromising: man dies but once, and after death, the judgment. You act as Christ acted. As Christ now acts.

The priest donned the vestments and evacuated his own personality. Yet Tom O'Donovan's Son of God was utterly different from John Cowburn's. The individuality was apparent as soon as each put on the alb. The code word for Tom O'Donovan's routine was reverent. He gathered up in lightly held panels the rear of the garment, and lowered it over his head so that the snowy cotton fell in soft symmetrical swoops. He eased the cincture around his waist and tightened it just so far. He stepped back to catch the full-length mirror and levelled the hem of the alb to exact mid-ankle height at every point. He tightened the cincture a little further. Then around both sides he stretched away the creases, tucking back the surplus cloth until he had a sharply regular double pleat. He checked the hem again in the mirror, gave a final tightening to the cincture and secured it against slippage.

John Cowburn was a Sydney man. He bounded in, only just on time, as though he were not long out of bed. He did a quick, crab-walk scrunch of the alb and tossed it over his head. He slung the cincture round his waist and yanked it tight. He raised his arms and plucked at the material around his chest so that it was loose there and allowed his rapid gestures unimpeded movement. He bounced the chasuble from the vesting table down over his body and swept on to the altar jagged and disarrayed.

When we were novices Michael Sullivan performed the variety of these Masses with detailed accuracy. He had been not six months at Watsonia when he found the gift one evening in a room at the far corner of the building normally used by re-treatants for their leisure. Around the four walls, broken only by the single door, were lines of soft vinyl armchairs. They were plusher, more inviting and harder to spring from than the un-adorned wood in the novices' recreation room. A large rectangular table in the middle of the room forced us to adopt a circle. Michael Sullivan, by turns garrulous and restless, stood facing the chairs. As a schoolboy he had been a sacristan, and a scholar even then of the Roman Ritual, and now something made him fall into gesture, in his side-of-the-mouth, disedifying way, and he said, "You know the way O'Donovan does it". He turned to the central table, and made to bend and kiss, with a protracted chasteness, this imagined altar, and then he rose, reluctantly, before the solemn turn to descend the altar steps. Someone in the chairs facing him laughed in recognition. Beside him someone turned to catch the joke. Michael Sullivan wheeled back and repeated his kiss. Gerard Healy cackled and then looked sideways. His harsh laughter and the swing of Michael Sullivan's gown were rippling around the circle. Novices eased around and stepped back so that they and others could see. Michael Sullivan alone remained at the table in the centre of the room.

The entire performance was in mime. It was an O'Donovan mass, perfect in style and pace, but taking about four minutes. Without hesitation, but without any loss of character, he cut as he went. The genuflections were stately but athletic, the back straight, the head at just the slightest reverential incline. When the climax of consecration came and the host was offered for adoration, the arms rose out from behind the skull and ascended in steady majesty, the thumbnails precisely even on the white disc, and the fleshy pads, the wrists and the elbows all approaching one another until the triangle was complete and held steady and the face of the Bread of Life was brought forward in a final tilt towards the worshippers. We held our breaths until he had eased away from this most sacred moment; then we gave way to open laughter. The rubrical observance, the reproductive skill was uncanny. "Now Cowburn," came the prompt. Michael Sullivan broke into a helter-skelter routine, all jerks and angularities and truncated movements. John Cowburn was an existentialist theologian. Michael Sullivan gave the rough edges, the discontinuities, the leaps, all the infelicitous motions of the wracked soul. It was all over in thirty seconds, a whole mass performed.

We laughed and clapped and were uneasy. This man, I thought, could never be a priest; such familiarity, at this age, with the sacred mysteries, must be an impediment: whatever might happen later on, a young man had to feel some hesitation and awe about this role. You did not play Christ as an after-dinner entertainment.

The Code of Canon Law had a prohibition on priests attending what it referred to as "*spectacula*". Each diocese had its own interpretation of this word. The laxer reading was that the *Folies Bergère*, racetracks and boxing stadiums could be an occasion of both sin and scandal for priests, and must be avoided. The stricter interpretation, favoured in Australia, was that all shows featuring live humans came under the interdict. Any association with theatre was out. Going to the pictures was allowable, at least in theory. The live performance was more unsettling. The terminology of the time also helped to sustain a distinction: "the pictures" offered one fewer dimension than "the movies". So I never went to the theatre while I was at Watsonia. As a scholastic I was sent out twice to the pictures. Tom O'Donovan, our Rector, decided that exceptions should be made to his general embargo for what he judged were the two significant films of the era. So I, and my fellow scholastics, were sent to see *A Man for All Seasons* and *The Sound of Music*.

The Jesuits however had a theatrical past. The masques and dramas composed and performed in their colleges were one of the originals that made up Baroque culture. We had an inheritance from men at centre stage of their era. So I went to ask Tom O'Donovan's permission to put on for our fellow Jesuits *Waiting for Godot*.

"I'll have to read it, Gerard. I don't know the play."

"It has an all-male cast," I said.

My second last year at school had been glutted with plays. It was not unconnected that the producers had invited in girls from the Marist convent. Lady Macbeth's gentlewoman began a correspondence with a second murderer, but no one came to grief. Then Rome heard of the enterprise. The Rector was admonished. He was apostrophised in the swingeing gerunds of Cato: *praxis abhorrenda est*. The practice is to be abhorred. So in my last year at school I became used once more to all-male productions. And women were more easily written out of *Julius Caesar* than out of *Macbeth*. Best if they were not there in the first place.

"Only men," I said to Tom O'Donovan, "and their ages can be anything."

"How many actors are required, Gerard?" he asked.

"Just five, Father. It wouldn't be too disruptive."

But, in pleading before Tom O'Donovan, only five actors was not a point in *Godot*'s favour.

Tom O'Donovan unbuttoned his gown and folded it across the back of a bentwood chair. He remained in full clericals. He stood in the middle of the hall facing the stage, leaning forward, his hands joined together with his thumbs crossed and his lips resting on his index fingers.

"When you're ready, Simon," he said to the pianist, "we'll take it again from "But when the breezes blow"."

Simon Campion crashed down on the keys. The baritone minced in.

"No," called Tom O'Donovan. "Not you, Sir Joseph. That's good. But all you sailors … You should be watching him, attentive to him, hanging on every word, so that you feel you really want to come in with your agreement. Take it again now. All eyes on him." He nodded to the pianist. "Very good, Simon."

The First Sea Lord confessed his nervousness again. The plentiful sailors, all roguishly masculine and jammed together on the narrow stage, gave him their exaggerated attention. "And so do his sisters and his cousins and his aunts." A ragged line of right fists plunged down in emphasis.

"And again!" called Tom O'Donovan.

The sailors bellowed.

"And an encore now!" shouted Tom O'Donovan.

Simon Campion hammed the keys, Sir Joseph Porter added a kick routine, the sailors swayed and roared and had to catch one another and began to have trouble with laughter.

"And once more."

Tom O'Donovan stood with his hands outstretched. His young men linked arms and carolled out in hysterical joy that "when the breezes blow we generally go below."

Alone in my room on the deserted floor above I felt the soles of my feet quivering. The notes rose and fell under Tom O'Donovan's flailing arm, and I felt the lash. I was absent from the communal act to which all were invited, the restorative raising of hearts and voices, all so happy and free from sin.

"I think not, Gerard," said Tom O'Donovan.

I couldn't acquiesce at once. "I would be grateful," I hesitated, "if I understood why you feel it not a good idea?"

"I wouldn't want you to be wasting your time."

"No. But this one seems a challenge."

"Ah Gerard, the Prefect of Studies agrees with me. I showed it to Father Gardiner. " Tom O'Donovan slapped the tight paperback of *Godot* against his palm. "This thing won't last."

"I understand."

"Have you thought of Sherwood Anderson? *Winterset*'s a marvellous play."

Tom O'Donovan was not a cheap joke. Without hypocrisy and according to his own harsh, narrow lights he was a father to his subjects.

Father Phillip was convalescing at Watsonia. He lined up every morning with the young men outside Tom O'Donovan's room, and took his turn. Tom O'Donovan, his contemporary, gave him his medication. He was happy then. He said Mass in the side chapel of Saint Stanislaus Kostka, the patron of novices.

He made his constrained way to the Canon, the shake visible in his hands as he blessed or touched wine and water. He came to the Consecration and bent over, the host looming against his small wire glasses. "*Hoc*," he breathed as the white disc filled his whole line of vision. His fingers shook a little, the contours of the white cloud shifted and were blurred, his spectacles began to steam up. "*Hoc*," he tried again, and paused. Kneeling at his back, I shifted on the altar step and peered round him. "This is …" I willed him to say. Above him the boy saint had his eyes to heaven in unshaken faith. Phil raised himself, took off his glasses, pulled a white handkerchief from his sleeve and polished the lenses. He readjusted. His fingers trembled round his ears and shivered their way to the bridge of his nose. Then his hands moved towards the host again and he leant down. But he did not touch it. He froze into a shaky rigidity. Not so much as an aspiration came from his lips. The Mass stalled.

I had to get help. I slipped from the chapel and tapped on Tom O'Donovan's door. "Father Phillip can't manage the Consecration, Father."

"Thank you, Gerard." Tom O'Donovan went to Phil's elbow. I stood back while he led him away. He helped him unvest, taking the garments as they were shaken loose. Phil left the chapel, a tuft of hair at his crown struggling from the oil, his gown sliding back from his neck, his oversize hands splayed across one another at his groin.

Tom O'Donovan clothed himself in the discarded vestments. Finished, he concentrated a moment before bowing to the crucifix and processing to the altar of Saint Stanislaus. His attention squeezed devotional warmth into this abruptly assumed, unfinished drama. He genuflected at the foot of the single step, strode up, bent over, and changed the friable disc into the Body of Christ.

Phil had a sister, a novelist. I was told, in more innocent days, that she had the balls of the family. Twenty years later when I

met her, she boomed at me, "Gerry Windsor, weren't you at
school at Terrace with my brother Phil?"

"No," I had to tell her. "I was never at Terrace. My uncle it
was. He was Gerard too. But he's dead."

We attended at least one Mass every day. I was still in my teens
or barely out of them. I sensed no shadow of death on me. Even
as a future notion death was insubstantial, for it existed only as
a prelude to the resurrection. Mass was an enactment of the
death and resurrection of Christ, but no living thing was seen to
die. Yet the Mass, perhaps an hour's worth of fussy devotion,
was, I was told and I believed, enacting a raucous slaughter, the
darkening of the earth and the one ached-for miracle of
resurrection.

I skewed my imagination to feel the drama. Christ was dying,
reverent or agitated, on the starched linen spread over nine
marble tops in our house. I was going with him, spectator and
actor and Christ himself, to be broken and offered to the Father.
Yet morning after morning I fought to hold my body upright,
my wrists barely scraping the bench fronts, my buttocks taut
against any easing on to the edge of the seat behind. Tom
O'Donovan distracted with his pageantry to the very moment
of the breakfast bell. John Cowburn's was the harder Mass to
take because he finished twenty minutes before the kitchen was
ready. I was thrown back into the continually scoured cave of
my own mind. It should have been the time of closest intimacy
with the transformed Christ, but I had been up for over two
hours, moving to a supernatural script, and now, more keenly
than at any other time in the day, I longed for animal relief. I
needed breakfast.

John Stamp waited in the kitchen. He was a coadjutor brother,
and so his province was the care of the less transcendent, more
flesh and blood man. John Stamp was a convert and a Londoner,

reputedly a veteran of the merchant navy, and I imagined he had knocked about. He had an arthritic limp, preferred the grubby look, and displayed little overt piety or anything but suspicion towards the egregiously pious young. I had no idea what had brought him to Catholicism and then to the religious life. I had little idea of what constituted goodness. John Stamp cooked eggs and coffee better than anyone else at Watsonia, and was up first in the morning, doing the rounds when there were lay retreatants in the house and the bell could not be rung and every room had to be woken individually.

John Stamp's nephew came to Australia. He was an actor. None of us had ever seen his films. He was not out on business, merely accompanying or chaperoning some model who was to do something at the Melbourne Cup. He took a taxi out to Watsonia to see his uncle. Visiting professionals were often invited to address us. Archbishop Young of Hobart had spoken about the first session of the Vatican Council, Dr John Billings had addressed us on birth control.

At a rapid hobble John Stamp brought Terence along the verandah to us. John Cowburn came with them. He knew about films and the theatre. He was in the chair. Terence was a little diffident, a little weary. We were all in black and wore our collars and gowns. Terence invited us to pull the bentwood chairs more into a semi-circle, out of their lines. He sat on a bentwood chair himself. "Well, what do I talk about?" he asked, fingers of one hand thrown up in the gesture of query, the other hand deep in a pocket and one leg thrown over his knee.

He talked about women. Not that I think we asked him that. Women had never been forbidden to us as a topic, but we saw little future in pursuing it. Terence Stamp just spoke about women he had worked with. Julie Christie was his favourite, he said. There was no actress like her.

"How's that?" prompted John Cowburn.

Terence Stamp turned a blank face, hardly looked at him, just stretched his neck a little. "She's the most beautiful woman in Britain," he said.

We were silent.

"Whereas Samantha was a bitch," he said. "Impossible to work with. I hated every moment of it."

"Do you have many disappointments, frustrations?" asked John Cowburn.

Terence rolled on his chair and ran his hand back from his forehead. He rolled his wrist forward and stopped, and rolled it again, making to start several lines of complaint. "Look, take the people you have to work with, the people you can't control. Your best work gets treated like shit." He pulled himself upright in his chair and began to act.

"I had this scene with Samantha. You remember it. We're about to make it together, and suddenly I realise I won't be able to manage it. One of those moments ... you know," and he looked first at John Cowburn and then swept across the rest of us, "one of those moments that happens to us all, all men, out of the blue, for no reason; we know we just can't manage it." He paused. "You know what I mean?" he asked, and fell back into his acting. "I got the look, I know it, on my face, that any man would see and recognise immediately. Just a shadow passing across, but it said it all. It was one of the best things I've ever done. Not sure that I could ever manage it again. You'll never see it," he said. "Fuckwit of an editor. All on the cutting room floor. The best thing I've ever done."

The following year I proposed *Godot* to Tom O'Donovan again. He gave permission. I had no idea why he'd changed his mind. We performed it for ourselves, just once, at Pentecost. We were invited to repeat it for the diocesan seminary at Corpus Christi College, Werribee. Their first year students had it as a text: *Godot* was the world without Christ. Minutes before the curtain rose their Prefect of Studies came backstage and beckoned me. He wanted three changes to the wording. Page 81, fifth last line, where Beckett had written "Who farted?" was now to be delivered as "Who belched?", page 82 last line as "this wretch" instead of "this bastard", and page 83, line one, as "Kick him in the guts" rather than "in the crotch". I was enraged but stony. We all had vows of obedience.

Before the lights were dimmed I peered through a hole in the curtain. The students were settling themselves, prepared. Estragon and Vladimir, shaken by the textual changes, started uncertainly. Murmurs rippled up from the auditorium. I peered again, screwing up my eyes against the dazzle of the footlights. Numerous heads seemed to be bowed. Suddenly throughout the room arms twitched and there was a rustle of fingers sliding over paper. It was pages being followed and turned. I pulled myself back into the prompt box, and coaxed and hissed my players through their stumbles and repetitions. Alternative readings floated in from the darkness.

"Charming evening we're having," said Vladimir.

I cringed against the inevitable riposte.

"Who belched?" roared Estragon.

From the auditorium there was a popping of fart noises and a ragged accompaniment of glee.

"It's this wretch Pozzo at it again," called Vladimir.

"Bastard, bastard," came the cries from the audience.

"Make him stop it," said Estragon, "kick him in the guts."

"Try the crotch, the crotch," called the seminarians.

I willed my players to hold on to their own lines of anarchy.

"I can't go on," said Vladimir. He paused. "What have I said?"

I panicked and jerked to my own text, racing for the place. "You're right," I said, half aloud.

"I can't go on like this," said Estragon.

"Yes," I whispered, "you're nearly there."

"Well? Shall we go?" asked Vladimir.

"Yes, let's go."

I urged the curtain down. I seethed with fury against those who closed in on the script and followed it dumbly. I seethed too against people who tampered with the script.

I walked on to the shrouded stage.

Stan Hogan stood bent, holding himself in, his head cocked to the side, his right hand up and open — a wave, a disowning of responsibility, a shrug, even a defiance, a caution.

"OK, OK, Vladimir," I said, "thanks for persevering."

Michael McKernan stood with his arms thrown wide, his chest out. He could have been about to bang heads together, or whoop with joy, or pump up and down in frustration. It was a last surge of action; he was haggard with sweat.

"Thanks, Estragon," I said. "You made it."

The three of us stood there, and for a moment we did not move.

In her eponymous autobiography of 1990 Jean Shrimpton devotes five pages to her Australian assignment of 1965. She remembered it, for her companion and herself, as a rough ride. Terry, she relates, was discomfited by the sense of disapproval coming from every direction. That, coupled with the fact that she was the one centre stage, "caused him to take off for San Francisco on the third day". At the end of her contract she joined him, and they went together to rest at a health farm near Los Angeles.

Dick Hall's Fable

It was the early 1990s. I was shouldering my way through the crowd, a child in hand, and I was looking for space to stand and see. I tried to drop my shoulders under raised glasses and I pulled my face back from streaming cigarettes and I did what I could to avoid brushing women's bodies. It was upstairs in the windowless functions bar of the Bellevue Hotel, and the heavy fug of sound rested above the islands of dense straining conversations. Amputated phrases fell ahead of me and behind me. "Ages … you been doing … the silly bastard … the September issue … what I've heard … time for Christmas … trouble with lawyers … split up … overseas … last night." I greeted and smiled but with my free hand I made indistinct gestures that meant I couldn't stay though I would have liked it but that I had responsibilities and had to be moving on. In fact I preferred to be passing unnoticed through the crowd and to be emerging on the other side of it. Where things would be freer. I elbowed into an opening and swivelled on my hips, and Dick Hall was profile on to me. "In Canberra, at the ANU …" he was saying. His face glistened with the delight of an uproarious believe-it-or-not. He was intent and didn't advert to me. I stepped sideways to ease myself on, and I caught another of Dick's facts. "Her father was Chief of the General Staff." I paused, my legs still spread, and I felt the child's hand wriggling, unsure of which opening he was supposed to follow.

"ANU was full of seminarians," Dick went on. "This was still those days. The place was crawling with them." He jerked his head around to take in all listeners.

I was nailed, there, in the middle of the floor. I was being told my own story. Or, perhaps worse, I was eavesdropping on it. I didn't know whether I wanted to be there or not. I half hoped Dick would realise this was my story and leave off. Or even hand it over to me. But no, I didn't want that. I thought he might get it wrong or obscure it, and I would be in the clear. Or, perhaps, cheated.

"She had a program," said Dick. "She was going to work her way through as many of them as possible. All those Sacred Heart students."

I stared at Dick, avoided anyone he was addressing.

"She did too. Seduced every one of them. It was well known around the place at the time."

I swung away into the press, biting my tongue. Every fact was wrong, but I could see where he'd got them from. She wasn't the daughter of the Chief of the General Staff — Dick should have thought more extravagantly for once — but I understood where he got the idea.

Still, it was the grand inaccuracy that I seized on. I smarted at being the butt of a story going the rounds. I burrowed away from that boisterous, harshly lit puppet stage. Dick had given no sign he knew it was my story, and that he had commandeered it. Very likely he had no idea. The poor — innocent as far as I knew — Sacred Heart students had no right to be included in such a mangled fable. They were a tighter, less troublesome lot altogether.

I broke through into the far corner of the room, a vacant space, and found some orange juice and poured some of it into two plastic mugs.

"Cheers," I said to the child. Our mugs bumped and the juice slopped across our fingers and on to the carpet. For once I took hardly any notice. What could I do with a runaway story like that? I was embarrassed and annoyed and nervous. *My* story, but a greased pig for all the control I had over it. Even if Dick's version were way off beam, there must be other versions out there, and some of them actually more accurate ones. Some of them might even feature me, by name.

I licked the back of my fingers, trying to get rid of the stickiness that I could feel glueing them together.

The child gulped the last of his juice, then inhaled the invisible drops. "Can we go now?"

I took in the room. "Follow me," I said. "Round the edges this time."

Some Jesuits never came to Watsonia, deliberately. Father Michael Scott left Campion Hall, my primary school, just before my eighth birthday, and I never saw him again, not even after I had joined the Society myself and although he was the Rector of Newman College, the Catholic residential college at Melbourne University. In the December 1967 issue of the now long-silent Jesuit magazine *Twentieth Century* I published a poem. "Separate Ways". It expressed the hope

> *That we'd have travelled as before, unfurled*
> *The same gay earth, and briefly pressed the one*
> *Horizon back, before we swerved to run,*
> *Each out along the highway of his world.*

It was not about Michael Scott. I had no thought of him. I had no one in mind. I gave way, stiffly and rhetorically, to that not unpleasant ache I always had for continuity, and then I countered it by saying there was no stepping twice in the same stream.

On the day that Campion Hall closed down, my last day there, when I was still a child of nine, I went out by myself on to the terrace over the front archway, a part of the school I had never been before, and I broke off a few leaves of the wandering jew that climbed there and I cried and cried. In my final weeks at Watsonia I sauntered up the back past the tennis courts, along the broad deep-gullied path that debouched on to the oval. Michael Scott was on the oval. Or I imagined he was. I couldn't make it out. He was not a figure seen here. He did not belong to the Jesuit life I had been introduced to here. Most Jesuits had been formed at Watsonia. Most Australian Jesuits, that is. Whereas Michael Scott had been a novice at Greenwich in Sydney. Then he had gone to Europe for twelve years. The scholastics in the year behind him, and forever afterwards, stayed in Australia for their training. Now he stood on the Watsonia property, but on its most remote, least distinctively religious edge. He was hatless and the sun drilled through his thinning hair. And he was alone. I walked towards him. I was nervous and I grasped the wings of my gown and flapped them across the front of my body as though I were swatting flies. Michael Scott was looking around him, his gaze beyond the perimeter of the oval, more towards the horizon or at least the crest of Preston Paddock and the flash of Grimshaw Street. He was frowning and smoking.

"You're off to Canberra," he said.

"Yes, so we've heard."

"It's a good move. It's the place to be."

It's a small town, I thought. We're being derailed. We should be in either Sydney or Melbourne. I had a helpless feeling of sliding into the second rate.

"The Society should be there," he said. "The national capital." He waved his cigarette at the obviousness of it. His fingers were browned and callused with nicotine.

No fervent Jesuit should be smoking, I thought. Displaying his weakness so openly.

"What about the university?" I asked. He should be reliable on that, I thought.

"Very good, very good," he said flatly. His head shook as though he were admitting the investigations had not been able to unearth anything negative. "I hear nothing but good of it. And many other advantages. The National Gallery, I'm told, is really going to be something."

I'd hardly been to a gallery in my life. I wasn't going to do Fine Arts.

In the motionless summer heat the compact line of smoke trailed between us. I rocked away from it and took a step back.

"It's the time to make the move," he said. "They say you're a talented crowd, and there's a lot of you."

"More than are coming on," I conceded.

"I'm all for it. I've argued it to the Provincial." For a moment his restless eyes held me directly. "This is exciting, a new step like this. Life in the Society isn't always exciting."

"No," I said. I did not yearn after excitement. I stopped swatting with the wings of my gown and I knotted them together.

Michael Scott started as the unseen flame in his cigarette reached his finger. He slid the butt forward to the very edge and looked at the ground before he let go. The butt disappeared into the uncut sprigs of early summer.

At Watsonia we drew apart into the desert awhile and prayed. It was what Christ had done before he started on his public ministry.

The property of Loyola extended over thirty acres. Only for a short distance on either side of the formal entrance gates was it walled. The rest of the perimeter was sown with mature cypress pines. The lower boles stretched to one another their misshapen spindles and their dry, unaligned false growths. Above this tracery, the grey-green needles closed up. They stretched for hundreds of yards at a time, turned at a precise right angle and glowered on again, unbroken in their constancy. Inside that boundary paths ran in concentric circles. At the rear of the property the paths frayed away into the open spaces of the Oval and Preston Paddock. The front boundary was where the burgeoning suburb of Watsonia advanced to meet us. For the five years of our residence the path here was being consolidated and christened. It was Father Gryst's Biblical Walk. Father Gryst was the Minister, the man in charge of the economy and practical business of the house. He was also the professor of Ontology: with an always smiling gruffness, with the bald dome of his forehead exactly analogous to the tight convexity of his stomach, he gave us precise Latin lectures on the universality and diversity of Being. After lunch, and by himself, he worked on his Biblical Walk. For at rest his mind toured and rambled through the Scriptures. Throughout the eastern Mediterranean and its hinterland he took note of the scenery and above all its vegetation. Then he shouldered his pick and shovel and strode to the front of the property and dug in all the plants, all the hardy growths of a land that ringed Jerusalem.

In the wilderness I will put cedar trees,
Acacias, myrtles, olives.
In the desert I will plant juniper,
Plane tree and cypress side by side.

Under the sharp, bone-dry edge of the February winds, Ted Gryst carried drums of water far beyond the reach of any hose or sprinkler system and irrigated Judaea and Galilee. His knowing and yet nervous smile never faded. The arc of his belly kept its perfect circularity. Most evenings, two by two, we passed along his Biblical Walk. In its farthest reaches the surface was packed clay and gravel, still raw and undwelt in. We passed along briskly, we never ambled on our walks, and we looked for our types and familiars. "I shall grow up like the cedar of Lebanon, I shall flourish like the palm tree, I hold out my arms like the plane tree." We could see little as yet that we recognised in the unpredictable growths that drooped or asserted themselves in their damp pans. Yet on we went, around and around again, trying to familiarise ourselves with a sacred landscape, exercising our vision so that it would be the only one we had.

Ted Gryst was in Rome, not the Holy Land, when his heart seized on him. Watsonia was being manoeuvred towards a sale when we were barely out of it. The Victorian government bought the building and the rear of the property: it was used by the Department of Corrective Services as a Training Centre for prison officers. The front of the property was sold separately. It was bought by the Catholic Education Office, and school buildings soon obliterated the Biblical Walk.

In Canberra we returned to the world. We went there after five years at Watsonia to study at the Australian National University. The Jesuits owned no property there as yet, so we boarded with the Dominicans, the Jesuits' one-time adversaries. The principle in their dispute had been the reconciliation of God's almighty power with humanity's free will. The Dominicans' bias was to allow nothing that might impugn the divine control. The Jesuits were determined to preserve human room to move. In 1968 however the Dominicans had just erected a three-storey, hexagonal priory to house a hundred men, and half their rooms were free. Money, and caution before the gathering uncertainties of the Church and the world of the 1960s brought Jesuits and Dominicans together. It suited both orders that the Jesuits should move into Dominican space.

We were guests at Blackfriars and the house was alien to us. We had to listen to the bells of the Dominicans' day, we were forced to share their seasonal fasts and abstinences, we came and went always by the back door. The board was paid, and we were treated with consideration, but we did not belong. We were Jesuits, and students at university, and we were just lodgers in someone else's home.

Blackfriars stood at the apex of a roundabout. Broad avenues radiated out from it, towards the Federal Highway and Sydney, towards Northbourne Avenue and the centre of the city, towards the rearing extravagance of Mount Ainslie. We left for university every morning at 8.45, in a white Kombi van, and we did not return till the day's lectures had ended at six o'clock. It was the way the Jesuits of our tradition had first encountered the world. In 1931, in Dublin, Michael Scott would bicycle in from the fastness of Rathfarnham Castle to University College, set by the open playground of Saint Stephens Green. For us it was a Jesuit community but not a Jesuit home we returned to. We had been sent away from Melbourne where there was a cloud of colleagues of all ages whose presence was always felt and frequently seen. We were pioneers in Canberra, and we had our own rules to make, or not to make.

For our refectory at Blackfriars we had the use of a spare room just inside the back door but adjacent to the kitchen.

At the end of March fifteen of us sat crowded over thin beef soup at the start of our evening meal. University life was still a novelty and we lived in a hum of excitement. We talked and joked loudly, high on the foreign air of a new world. The last of the speckled liquid was spooned away, the servers rose and stacked the plates, and in that precise moment following the disappearance of the old and empty, before the new start, there came the nervous but sustained tapping of a spoon against a glass tumbler. We subsided and looked around. Our Superior, Father Cornelius Finn, cleared his throat and sniffed, more than once, and when we were quite silent he unfolded a small sheet of paper and read aloud. "Ad Maiorem Dei Gloriam. Dear Fathers and Brothers in Christ, I wish to inform you that Father Michael Scott has been released from his vows and has left the Society. Father Scott leaves us with the fullest approval and best wishes of his Superiors. Father Scott has left Australia and is in a Benedictine monastery in Belgium. We are all deeply grateful to him for all he has done during his forty years in the Society, and we pray that God's blessing may be on him in his future life. I remain, yours sincerely in Christ, F. P. Kelly S.J." Then Father Finn turned and nodded to the servers and our routine started up again.

"Jesus!' said Terry McEwen, "Sends us to Devil's Island, then skips."

"To the Benedictines! What's come over him?"

I shared the flippancy, but I was shaken. It was the age of departures, but not of men who had been in the Society for forty years. Priests had been known to go, but they were young, or they had been lost overseas for years, or they were sick, nervy men who could not be fruitfully accommodated. Michael Scott was in his late fifties, active, a Rector, and a man of both high profile and prestige. This kind of departure cut jaggedly across the nerves of security and fellowship.

Yet for me the blow was softened by the rider about a move to a Benedictine monastery. Such a step meant there was no public denial of the religious life. Jesuits had always been free to leave the Society to join the Carthusians: a Charterhouse was the only form of religious life conceded to be more exacting than the Society of Jesus. Maybe a Benedictine monastery could be substituted in certain circumstances. After all, Michael Scott had artistic interests, more in a Benedictine tradition than a Jesuit one. We heard nothing more. I alone had ever known the man, and that was between my fifth and eighth birthdays. The connections were lost, or at least frayed.

I was in the Chifley Library at ANU, in the Current Periodicals room. All the up-to-date gossip and stoushes and writerly try-ons decorated the walls. The effect was bright and pristine, and I could skim or immerse myself at will. The cornucopia waiting at my back, I began with what I was used to. From the newspaper rack I lifted the *Age* on its wooden roller and waved it down like a falling flag to the low reading table. I spread it open.

There was no one else there. I cropped my way across the sheets and I came to the item on page nine. "Australian Ex-Priest Marries in Ireland," the brief notice was headed. She was a writer and a widow. Mary Lavin. The name meant nothing to me. The item did not flesh out the story. That was the end of it. He was gone now. My first Jesuit. Irrevocably gone.

The sexual urge was never to be the sexual imperative. It was the only sacrifice whose wrench I felt, and continued to feel, achingly, month after month. It was the only sacrifice. Moreover it was the blind, promiscuous urge that hurt. Not the collaterals of sexual abstinence that we were told were part of our sacrifice. At the age of eighteen, long tagged by five younger siblings, I had no ambition for children. The longing and fulfilments of the patriarchs were not emotions I shared. There was no pain in renouncing my right to have children of my own, to have my name carried on. To live always familially, as the head of a household, was so remote from any predisposition I had that it was entirely without magnetic attraction. Those kinds of feelings seemed to me peculiarly Old Testament ambitions, of the kind sweepingly abrogated by the more spiritual dispensation of the New. So thoroughly had Christ refined Moses that I, a product of a two millennia tradition, no longer even felt such temptations of the flesh. Sex, however, the raw primal tumult, was impervious and implacable.

So many of our rules, and particularly our restrictions, were designed to corral it. The senses were the windows of the soul, and they were bolted against the anarchic, the combustible matter of sex. In the beginning, and the relaxation was very gradual, we saw no radio or television or newspapers or secular books or journals. Our only correspondence was with our immediate family. We went beyond the property only to the doctor or dentist or Jesuit churches, or on villa and excursions and that always in groups. We had the *ne tangas* rule.

I would say it was a very chaste house. I knew of no overt sexual activity at Watsonia. I never masturbated. I never had. I had never seen or touched a naked woman. I had never more than kissed a woman. I presumed much the same of my colleagues. I never discussed sex, either my experience or fear of it, or my strategies against it. I did not mention the subject with the Master of Novices, nor with any of my subsequent spiritual fathers. The Master of Novices treated it forthrightly in his lectures on the Jesuit life when he came to the vows of Poverty, Chastity and Obedience. It was a matter of vigilance and effort. "Many is the Scholastic," he said, "who married the nurse who looked after him in hospital." I would, I knew, have liked the experience of that temptation. But I never had to go to hospital.

I could control my imagination, as long as the shutters stayed clamped across the windows of my soul, and as long as my resolution held. I was thrown, however, and so a little frightened, when I was brushed by the passing of young women. It was inevitable. We had a garden party in December every year. Jesuits had sisters, I had one myself. They came party-dressed to a gala occasion. They were bright with the unusualness of it and heady with their own desirability, and, I suppose, their own desires among this evanescent body of black-clothed young celibates being introduced and waiting on them. The laughter was high strung, the limits of familiarity were probed. It all lasted three hours. The *clausura* was lifted just enough to allow the guests to pass across the *via max* into the chapel. Then Benediction and they were gone. Yet for a long time that lifted barrier could not be repositioned tight and prohibitive. I went to my prayers and my reading and my meals, my head a swirl of the tight sheen of material, and samples of colour for which my Jesuit life had no use, and the diminuendo of higher-pitched voices streaming into my house.

Ten months after taking vows, nearly three years after entering the Society, we sang carols with the Sisters of Mercy in their novitiate at Rosanna, just a few stations down the line. In the bus I wore my good suit, the one in which I had taken my vows, and I carried my vow gown carefully folded across my lap. We were at the convent by half-past seven, and we stood waiting in the bright summer night on the gravel outside the chapel. We all put on our gowns and hitched and balanced them with our thumbs so that they sat evenly on the shoulders. I talked, in a distracted, temporising way, and stood balancing myself on the edge of the grass, now and then stabbing the ball of my foot against the gravel to keep myself from toppling. I had no interest in the buildings or the grounds, and there were no people to be seen other than ourselves.

We awaited instructions from our Rector, Tom O'Donovan, who was to conduct and had already visited the convent for a rehearsal. He came from the sacristy door, smoothing down the ironed folds of his long ornately laced surplice. Clapping his hands with a sharp gentleness, he called, "All right now, men, the sisters are ready for us." We looked sober and made final adjustments to our appearance and filed into the chapel. I stared straight ahead and held the stapled pages of the program in my joined hands. Tom O'Donovan directed us on to the sanctuary, just one step up from the level of the congregation, and we took our places in two wings, not quite a semi-circle, across the base of the altar. We were in no order, tenors, basses, baritones all mixed together, for this was neither a concert nor a liturgical event but a familial celebration of Christmas. There were perhaps forty of us, and we had to go two-deep in places. I was towards the middle of the arc and I felt the tension, quite equal and opposite, as taller men resisted and then gave in to their obligation to fall back, and those on the ends faced one another across the sanctuary moving just one of their feet or turning their hips so that their eyes might go down into the nave. In the centre I should have held my head up and looked spontaneously ahead. Yet I shrank from some brazen directness in the gesture, and my eyes hovered over the side wall before they slipped uneasily towards the nave. The nave was wholly taken up by choir stalls and the stalls were full. The nuns were in black as we were in black, except for the white veils of the novices which ran in two brimming crests across the front of the choirstalls. Buoying the novices and packing them round was the unbroken depth of black, recently professed young nuns and in the rear their senior sisters. Even from the centre of our semi-circle I could distinguish no individual. The women were side-on to me and looked steadfastly ahead. Their veils fell, shielding their profiles and in the irregular tremble of the booklets and the generous sleeves of the habits all I ever glimpsed was the sleek flourish of gloves.

Tom O'Donovan took his stand beside us, on the very edge of the sanctuary step, in line with the front of the stalls on the gospel side. Any position between the two choirs would have been awkward, but everyone had some view of him there. He spoke to the women a few quiet words, inaudible to us, and nodded to the nun at the console. His hand began its tight undulation, and then jerked into a crisp beat. I hesitated and missed the note. I wanted to hear the voices of the women. But they were lost in the surge of Jesuit voices around me. My brothers caught me as they stormed to the attack. Briskly we bobbed along the line, "O come, O come, Emmanuel". As the cries went up from the sanctuary I heard in my own voice and the voices beside me, desire and challenge. We lingered over the longed-for name, leaning back and circling around each syllable as it sprang from our throats. Our own cries were all I saw and heard. We came to the end of the verse and drew in for the quick, long leap of the perfect fifth from G to D. I knew I couldn't make it and I sensed the hesitation elsewhere. We vaulted, and it was ragged.

"Rejoice, Rejoice," came the sweet, high refrain from the

nave. They were voices, they were notes we never heard, and I faltered, not knowing whether this unattainable pitch was a cry of triumph or of challenge or in fact a help-up. "Rejoice! Rejoice! Emmanuel shall come to thee, O Israel." Only when my lips had met and parted on the soft joints of the name, and the simple monosyllables had pranced by, could I reassert myself in the deep shudder of that final "Israel".

After that the women's voices leaped above us again and then appeared to fall away silenced, and then again rose. I could see no mouths, no throats. Just the slackening or tensing of white or black veils. Tom O'Donovan stood between us, and the women must have turned at least their eyes sometimes towards him. But we were not going to see or, most likely, be seen. I felt myself and the men beside me relax into the pummelling of the notes. We leant against them and they softened and we rolled with them, carolling the appearance of that strange but archetypal family. "Unto us a boy is born," we tripped. "Omega and Alpha he!" I fired my acclamation into the modest vault. "Let the organ thunder, while the choir with peals of glee doth rend the air asunder."

The dark mass of the nuns flowed out through the bottom door and disappeared. Then we ourselves filed out and were served tea and sandwiches and biscuits. Several of the senior nuns, who knew Tom O'Donovan, looked after us. We were all on the bus by half-past nine, and home well before ten.

Yet garden parties and carols were encounters between family formations, and each withdrew in order. When I was alone — and it happened — I was not nearly so sure how steady I was. I caught the train in from Watsonia to the ophthalmologist in Collins Street, and by the time I had done, it was peak hour and the red toast-rack carriages on the Hurstbridge line were crowded. I sat where I could. There was a girl beside me, there was a girl opposite me. Our eyes touched, or our thighs touched.

My heart raced, but the confusion was as great as the excitement. I could not help the light brushes and the pressure, but I was almost certain there was more to them than the confines of space and the motion of the train. If we were to be that close in any case, there was no harm in easing my legs a little wider apart, and letting my dull gaze around the carriage and through the window linger where it might pick up another pair of eyes. Just slightly, just briefly. And was it the swaying or was it the narrow range of views or was there some reciprocation when I felt others' eyes and legs rest on mine? Passengers got on and off, they moved apart or moved up closer. I was hardly fixing my attention on one individual. I was spinning in some new element, not registering any unique object. I felt a foreign tide of blood right across the dry shallows of my chest. I couldn't unblock a swollen hum along the passages of my ears. I was confined in this compartment by both necessity and choice. All the way, virtually to the end of the line, I had to ride, and ride out, this protean, ever-present pull on me. Only when I had stepped off on to the illuminated bareness of Watsonia station, clanged the door behind me, and not looked back to see if anyone were willing to hook my eyes in that bold, safe, last moment, only then did the tide begin to recede and my ears begin to register normally again. I climbed away from the train, down across the stony gutters of pink clay and smudged sand, over the fraying margins of Watsonia Road and on to the concrete footpath for home. The straight line ahead, the sharp, ruled rectangles of cement, and I was steadied. Resolute, relieved strides, and the tips of the cypresses coming into view over the stretch of bungalows, and the fug, the whirlpool, was sucked away. In the thickening evening I shook my head and trembled at the danger of it.

It was not an intellectual problem for me. There was no point in discussing it. I just had to keep going. Frequently, especially in the early mornings when I was woken abruptly and had to rip myself from bed before even the briefest experience of luxuriating there, so frequently then I felt winded at the thought that this ache would be permanent and unrelieved and I would not be able to do anything about it. Not once. Never. Never. I shut my imagination hard against the horizon and thought of today, today. One day at a time. I would get older, and then old.

Five years after it all began, January 1968 we reached university, in Canberra. This was the world. It was a dry, burning February, and the archbishop was asked to dispense us from the obligation to wear the sweaty bands of plastic, our collars. He allowed us to wear open-necked white shirts. So we never appeared at the university, as we had always done for lectures at Watsonia, in full clerical garb. As the year developed the white of our shirts was coloured in, and the black of our trousers was bleached. We argued, or were privately critical, about this slide away from the prescriptive norms of black and white. Yet removing our identity markings must have been a first gesture of assertion. It had no effect on the small student community of the Australian National University. We were defined as a group, and primarily by one feature: we arrived at the university all together in a Kombi van. The vehicle was known, not by us, as the Chastity Chariot. We were professional celibates. That was our hallmark.

We were vowed as much to obedience, but that made no public impression. It was of no interest to anyone but ourselves. Yet the two obligations interlocked. The white knuckle of discipline or the loose limbs of freedom. The force of individuals held us or let us drift. At Watsonia we had been shadowed by a crowd of witnesses, sagacious, strict, exemplary, escorting us through each twenty-four hours. At Blackfriars there was just one replaceable priest able to attend to barely more than our nighttime care. The sole statutory authority and experienced model for our lives was, at first, Con Finn, a hand-wringing Irishman of cautious precision, and, after him, Brian Murphy, a gentle, bumbling, simple Australian given to bewildered apoplexies. Each morning we were tumbled out of our chastity chariot on to an Australian campus, and it was 1968, the age of Aquarius, and fair liberty was all the cry, and the man left idle behind had no notion of where his charges were during the day except that they roamed a world that was a dark continent to him.

Oh, we were in small classrooms cosseted by sun-drenched shrubbery, or in shy groups where everyone was Mister or Miss, and there was an abnormal proportion of other religious — Missionaries of the Sacred Heart and Christian Brothers and Sisters of Mercy and Ursulines and Sisters of the Good Samaritan.

Yet it was a new world for all that. We entered it at an enthusiastic run, but small threads caught us, or maybe caught me, and twitched me out of the sure line of my progress. In the Tank, the sunken bowl of a lecture theatre that accommodated any large Arts group, Fred Langman lectured to more than a hundred on *The Waste Land*. He experimented with a tutorial method. He gave us the beginning of "The Fire Sermon".

"What does this mean?" he asked. " 'The river's tent is broken; the last fingers of leaf clutch and sink into the wet bank.' "

The Tank was cool and dark. No one moved.

"Yes, I'd like an answer," he nodded dryly.

Penny Chapman raised her hand.

Fred Langman leant forward. "Yes?"

Penny Chapman's voice was ringing. There was no constraint. "It means the loss of virginity," she told everyone.

Fred Langman held his pose. "I see," he said on a rising note.

I kept my eyes low on the seat in front of me. Questions and worries swarmed through me. I was stretched out, immobile. Fred Langman did not release me. Was she right? What did he think of the answer? Was he going to call for agreement or dissent? Nominate someone to comment? Already I was embarrassed. Right or wrong, such a remark being made so publicly

... and by a girl. Especially when it was surely not the obvious interpretation. Above all because it was personal to me. People, I cringed, must be thinking of me, looking at me. Because here I was defined by virginity.

"The word 'broken' ...," said Penny Chapman, "the over-hanging leaves that block progress along the stream, they have been burst through and pushed aside."

The brash explicitness of it chilled me.

"I see, I see," said Fred Langman still. "Let us go on. 'The nymphs are departed.' Why is that?" He sent a quizzical half smile towards Penny Chapman. I could see the challenge to her to continue her logic. But she was silent. " 'The nymphs are departed'," repeated Fred Langman.

We retired into the library. We established customary places and patterns for our breaks.

We settled on companions whose desks we stood by and to whom we whispered. I worked but I was not whole-hearted. There were distractions in the air such as I had never felt. Up and down the stairwell that I used passed Bettina Arndt, bright and splendid. She seemed to shake out her perfume there so that the field of her force lingered on till it was renewed by her next, not long-delayed, ascent or descent. I had pointed out to me a man who was in thrall to her, but his step lacked her spring and he was too irritatingly at her elbow, and I was told there was something clandestine about the pairing.

At the bottom of the stairwell, on the lowest level, were the men's toilets, and there were two graffiti there which were never erased. The pungent, badly ventilated air seemed to etch them more sharply. "Susan shags on Sheridan sheets," I read on the pebbled divider. I hadn't heard the verb for five years. Memories flickered of a heavy bird on a leaning pile in the Lane Cove River, and my pointing it out, and then raised eyebrows and sniggers. I was affronted now by this graffiti, not amused. There was a grossness somewhere, but the harsh alliteration of the phrase was insistent. It bucked away in my mind.

The graffiti on the end door, the more private cubicle, intrigued rather than irritated me. It was subtler. I almost expected an exclamation mark, but it got its effect without punctuation. I wanted to see the face of the writer. "Wendy Bacon," he had written, "is a virgin". I presumed the writer thought the idea absurdly unlikely. It certainly seemed so to me. No libertarian student agitator would be a virgin. I suspected the writer and I had different views about this improbability. Virginity was a fine thing, a preferable state. It was the last thing I would expect in someone who was a defiant publisher of what was legally obscene. It would have been nice if such a claim about Wendy Bacon were true. But it couldn't be true. It was just a joke. Virginity was probably a swear word to the writer. His witticism worked as a slur. Though why he wanted to blacken Wendy Bacon I had no idea. Opponents would hardly make that sort of claim about her. It was a joke, without much meaning. Any unlikely combination was fair game.

It was impossible to go into the men's toilets without the graffiti teasing me. Even if I did not see them, they were as insistent as the rank air of piss and wet cigarette ends and urinal crystals and modulations of expelled gas.

On Saturdays or Sundays now, we went on villa. We drove out in the Kombi to the Brindabellas or the Cotter Dam or Uriarra Crossing or Kambah Pool, places that others before us had discovered and named, and still frequented. Going on villa was optional. Two scholastics played football for the university. Others went to watch them. Another walked out of sight of Blackfriars, took a taxi to the airport, then a flight to Sydney, and a further taxi to Randwick. When he ran into his surprised father in the betting ring, the scholastic put his fingers to his lips.

"Don't tell mother," he said. He was only a little late back for tea at Blackfriars at six o'clock.

I had a sister living in Canberra. She was single and had only just arrived there. I asked Father Finn if she could come on villa with us in the van. He asked me to come back, said he would think about it. I returned to him the next day.

He stood, hunched over, and rubbed the tips of his fingers against his upper teeth. "Come in, come in," he nodded. "Close the door."

I waited.

He poked his glasses further up the bridge of his nose and gave a convulsive blink. "It's very delicate, you see. It's very thoughtful of you as a brother, and I'm sure there'd be no harm, none at all." His joined hands sprang back on to his teeth. "The trouble is …", and the words were slow and tense with his concentration, "we're known, we're known. But nobody would know she's your sister. Nobody who just saw you." He leant forward further with each sentence, and his head bobbed in appeal to the reasonableness of what he was saying.

I saw no room to move.

He had a further, happy inspiration. "Besides, she's *your* sister. We mustn't forget she's no one else's sister." He drew back and tapped the tips of his fingers together.

I knew that he smoked, and his fingers were trembling for the cigarette, but he never smoked in front of us. A cigarette now was the only thing he had in mind. He had given his ruling. He just wanted me to leave.

I fought down the growl of my annoyance. The blocks of his logic were impermeable. A dry stone wall. He stood behind it anxious and in pain.

I could not probe or push him any further. "No, Father," I said. "Thank you." I was steely and ungracious, in a righteous, impotent fury. I turned my back, raging at all timid meanness of spirit. Behind me I heard the ratchet unwind, opening the

window. There was a moment of fire in the air, then smoke
easing away.

I fell in love. Or perhaps I just fell. In September of my second
year at university I came to Sydney, we all came, to meet the
Jesuit General. My father was driving me, and some other
scholastics, north along Crown Street. We had stopped at the
Stanley Street lights when I saw a girl. I wound down the
window and called her name and opened the door and leaped
out and stood before her and said hello and slipped back into
the car, all before the lights changed. "She's someone we're in
classes with," I explained. My father let in the clutch and said
nothing. Years later he told me that he knew then, at that
moment, that it was only a matter of time.

It was December of that same year, 1969, that I arranged my
departure from the Society. In Canberra I had spoken to Father
Kelly, the Provincial. Later he had written to me, telling me to
go. After our exams at ANU my colleagues and I returned to
Melbourne for the Christmas holidays. One night, early in the
month, I was allowed a Jesuit car to drive from Studley Park
Road in Kew to the Provincial's residence in Power Street,
Hawthorn. It was a bluestone Victorian mansion, and I went up
the back stairs and waited in a small room where the brothers
were at recreation watching a western on television. Even as the
hooves thundered and the dust rose and the bullets ricocheted
off the rocks, Jack O'Callaghan made slow, genial conversation.
He sat half on to the set, and seemed compelled to look away at
it only when the action fell silent. The chase and the duel failed
to change the tenor of his interest.

"And how do you like Canberra?" he asked.

"Well, it's a big change after Watsonia," I said.

He watched the mayhem on the screen for a few seconds, then
swivelled his head and shoulders again. "Do you see any of the
politicians?"

"They come to the university and talk. Some of them. Just occasionally."

Jack O'Callaghan bobbed his head sagely.

I felt all the transience of the intruder. Surely he wondered what I was here for? Maybe he knew. Probably did, I thought. Scholastics didn't lob in at this hour for trivial matters. I was on a padded bench along a wall and felt I was on the outer edge of everything. A man on the screen stumbled forward clutching his stomach. The ribbons of his tie dangled, and yanked him forward.

"Father Murphy enjoying lots of laughs is he, brother?" Jack O'Callaghan grinned at his own gentle, heavy-handed mischievousness. Brian Murphy was a prey to breathy, nervous guffaws.

"We've got a few funny men. We keep the jokes up to him."

The man with the smoking gun bent down, picked up the prone cowboy's hat and laid it across his face.

"Last rites," said Jack O'Callaghan.

A door opened. The Provincial, Father Peter Kelly, came out, nodded quietly and we both went in.

I saw only him. The rest of the room was merely unvarnished darkness. Father Kelly sat by a soft lamp. He had said I should go, but now he suggested alternatives. "You could defer university and teach for a year or two in Perth," he said.

The light spun, a small planet inside the disc of gloom. I felt the sorrow of it all, the desolation of this frequent office of Peter Kelly. It was a pang of gratitude that I felt towards him. But now, after seven years of instinctual and trivial obedience, the stick in the old man's hand, I was suddenly hardened against haphazard, ad hoc swerves in my life.

"That would be putting off the problem," I said.

I just wanted to go on at university within or outside the Society. Perth was a distant emptiness where I had no one and no reason for being. Leaving the Society in Canberra would not be the chaotic severance that going to the West would be. The offer strengthened my resolution. "I think I should leave," I said, and I heard the concession in my voice, agreeing with his own first judgment, letting him off the hook. Yet I could not bring myself to try the words, "I want to leave".

Father Kelly was still, the spinning light slowing down, funnelling across the fine-china bones of his face and the thin black pen mounted in his fingers.

"I think it's the only thing to do," I said.

"Very well," he answered, and the pen twitched a moment before he stilled it. "May I offer a word of advice."

"Of course." I was surprised that we were going beyond the formalities of the occasion. I crossed my legs and hugged my knees.

"You have a tendency which could come against you. I think you should watch it." His voice was calm and solicitous. He spoke as though offering a going-away present.

I thought he was speaking of chastity. I thought the rules and my own nature there were clear to me. I waited for his gloss on the little I believed he knew of me.

"You can be very abrasive," he said. "You take up a position or hold a point of view — which may very well be correct, or at least arguable — but you get people's backs up by the way you propose and fight it." He let the charge sink in, and rolled his pen between the fingers of two hands.

The accusation landed, unsighted, out of the darkness. The hurt flailed through me.

"A number of your fellow scholastics," he went on, "quite independently, have mentioned this to me. I should say too that it was not in the context of any general ill-will towards you. They spoke with real regret that so many fine qualities should be spoilt by this occasional tendency."

He was sincere. He had the reins on his own note of regret.

He was the pastoral priest, even friend, not the religious superior. But the charges detonated in me like delayed shrapnel. I nodded. I nodded, thinking *Who was this? Why did they never say this to my face? This is hardly what I have come here for.*

I said nothing. Peter Kelly had said all he was going to say. He switched to kind practicalities. "Go on the villa, at least for part of the time. Book your train ticket for when it suits you. We'll send the documentation after you." His pen lay on the table.

Past the shadow I began to notice filing cabinets and the unprimped spines of the primers of the Christian vocation: the bound, mission-brown volumes of old Jesuit catalogues: the loose, multi-coloured, current issues from each Jesuit province around the world, leaning and sliding towards the waiting gap on the shelves.

Peter Kelly rose with me. Sorrow and sympathy circling the desk. Peter Kelly himself, five years later, wrestling with the angel as I had never done, and then walking away. Out I stepped into the shriek and whine of passions and the drift of gunsmoke, the brothers barely noticing. Simon Campion waiting, his hand outstretched for his turn with the car keys, fidgeting over his own unrevealed business with the Provincial, wriggling his toe, starting to edge towards a fitful instant of illumination and decisiveness and his own departure three years later. I went out and down, past the parked car. I had to walk this time. I turned left into Power Street and headed north.

Temperamental incompatibility with the vows, I answered, whenever the question was asked. Countless times and predictably enough. I would have meant the vow of chastity, but Peter Kelly had alerted me to other limitations — or was that too accepting of the ethos? — To other strengths perhaps. Other tendencies at any rate.

It must have been very hard, leaving, people said. It wasn't, and that relative ease was a caution and a worry. There were factors enough to cushion the move. I was young, turning twenty-five as I left. I was not losing my companions. Of the twenty-three who had entered on 1 February 1963, twelve took vows at the end of the two years, and were still there three years later. One already had a degree, one had never matriculated, so only ten of our originals went to Canberra. By the summer of my departure five had gone. There was no interruption to the degrees we were doing, the student body was small, we were enrolled in the same subjects, we went to live in the same residential colleges. Those still in the Society came and went according to the old routines. They were advised, we learnt, to keep a courteous distance from those who had left them. We were not to be invited to visit Blackfriars, and I certainly never went there again. The attitude was understandable; it was hard not to see us as defectors, and the bad apples policy came into play. Exceptions were made; Michael McKernan was a man who inspired love, and the Superior, Brian Murphy, loved him, and Michael went back and played squash at Blackfriars every week. The coolness hardly registered with us. We were given $200 each, and the living allowances from Commonwealth Scholarships, which we all had, now reverted to us and no longer went into Jesuit consolidated revenue. Father Murphy informed the Department of National Service that Terence John McEwen who had been balloted in for Service but had been granted the exemption allowed to theological students was no longer covered by that exemption. Terry registered as a conscientious objector, and when his case was heard, there was considerable discussion of Aquinas and study of the just war theory, and on this ground his objection was upheld. We sold menswear in David Jones on Friday night and Saturday morning, and bought bomb cars, and went to the college balls, and within two or three years most married, and only then, separately, did we disperse interstate, reversing the patterns of ten years before.

That I could have done it so lightly shadows the whole seven-year enterprise. Had I ceased to believe in the Jesuit, or even the Christian vocation? Or was my belief suspect in the first place? No, not the latter. I had entered clear-eyed, with resolute intensity of purpose. All through my schooldays, the compulsion never left me. I just procrastinated and wriggled and said I had not made up my mind.

The call to the priesthood was formally enunciated twice a year at school, just often enough to keep the prickle turning in my conscience. Monsignor McGovern came on behalf of the archdiocese of Sydney; the Jesuits had no alternative but to admit him. He addressed every class on vocations, and boys who were interested further were invited to see him privately. He had curly ginger hair and strong glasses and no sense of humour and was not well suited for either boys or pedagogy. You were exposed when you were called out of class to see him. Some boys made appointments just to break the routine of work or to provoke incredulous laughter and mockery when they were summoned. I had no idea what they said to him. But the class could always distinguish the genuine enquirer, and when he was called there tended to be a ripple of hisses and feigned contempt. I had little to say to Monsignor McGovern. I had no alternative but to see him. I was thinking of being a priest; that was the only requirement. But not his sort of priest. I had to say to him, "At the moment I'm thinking of entering the Society".

"Of course. After all they're the priests you know. But think about Springwood. It might suit you better."

"Yes, Monsignor."

"After all, you never know where God might want to lead you."

"No, Monsignor."

In a school with more than twenty Jesuits on the staff, the invitation to join them was always there, the eyebrow forever cocked: What about it? The matter was made explicit during the annual retreat. For two days the school was silent, or at least bound to silence, and as I sifted through the broad tables covered with mounds of Catholic Truth Society pamphlets, or looked with an undeniable keenness towards this year's talk on chastity, I felt the cold pressure of the decision to be faced again.

Yet, if it was a compulsion, it was a cultural not a personal one. Or how was that to be distinguished from what is referred to as the promptings of the Holy Spirit? For the compulsion was towards what my whole outlook showed me as the finest and most useful and noblest thing I could do with my life. My parents gave no overt directions. The motivation was actually religious, and to that extent relatively pure. Christ looked upon the young man and loved him, and said to him, "Go, sell all you have and give to the poor, and come, follow me". It was dedication and the spirit of sacrifice and a belief that hardship was a fit sharing of the way of the cross for a cause that was, in the last analysis, the only one that mattered, and that would finally triumph.

The love of God was a phrase that had always been to hand, throughout my life. To love the Lord thy God with thy whole heart and thy whole mind and thy whole soul. The obligation, and presumably the orientation and the vocation, was so comprehensive. I strove to love him in the ways I had been instructed. Yet the difference between this love and any other love I knew or knew of was profound. I might be called to love God with my whole heart, but my love for him had no trace of that spontaneous urge and emotional tide that was inseparable from any other love I knew. Except perhaps on that spring evening when I decisively withdrew my opposition to the idea of entering and the tumble of resolution and euphoria broke over me. Or as it did when I was a novice, in the quiet of the half hour of prayer, in the fading of the day, just before dinner. Though with greater infrequency as the months passed. Yet, for all these moments, I feared some natural interpretation of the workings

of my soul. Even at the height of my fervour I knew there was
a secular, even commonsense, explanation for the gushes and
the constrictions of the life of prayer. As soon as I learnt about
Occam's Razor it forced itself into my hand whenever I wondered about the emotions of my spiritual life. If the rises and
falls of my euphoria could be explained without immediate
recourse to God, they should be. The simpler explanation suf-
ficed perfectly. Grace built on nature. It did not pre-empt or
displace it. The axioms trembled in balance in my mind. They
freed and propelled me. They also made it harder to know
whether I was in touch with God. Being in love with him then
could hardly be an issue.

It was a drift really. Away from the desert where the deprived
senses let in nothing and concentrated the mind on rigour and
endurance, and the last end of it all. Away too from Mount Tabor
and Christ transfigured and the vision of heart-swamping
splendour. The insistence of the other world faded. Whereas the
question of that other world had not yet arisen in those undergraduate years. Its reality was the later problem. Once it surfaces
there sets in the unbreakable, harrowing circularity. Do you
doubt because you let go God's insistent presence? Will the
doubt now forever paralyse the reawakening nerves? You hope
or you despair.

Scattered Leaves

So, what happens in the break-down? Certainly my break-down. But numberless other leaves falling, and birds beating away from the heaving ocean, and arms stretched this way and that in longing. Trajectories we can speculate on. Crossings right to the farther bank.

A Spoiled Priest

On my grandmother's verandah, just inside the half-door which led to the garden and the river and the Murrurundi hills, was a shelved hallstand with books that had been in the family since my grandmother's childhood. Painted Edwardian covers done in blind, Louise Mack, *Claude Lightfoot* by Father Francis Finn. I read *Claude Lightfoot*, one of a series of boys' adventures by an American Jesuit. At the end of each book the hero signalled his intention of becoming a priest. That was straightforward. It was another book that intrigued, and mystified, me. Its title page said, "Sheehan, Rev. P.A. … D.D., author of "The Triumph of Failure" "My New Curate", etc., *A Spoiled Priest & Other Stories*, with nine illustrations by M. Healy, London, T. Fisher Unwin, 1905, Unwin's Colonial Library." The book had two inscriptions. In pencil, across the top of the front free endpaper, was the owner's name "Miss Imelda Dooley, Murrundi". The misspelling confused me. On the same page, but vertically upwards along the hinge, and in ink, was the presentation inscription: "Remember me, Till darling, Dot". The owner's signature was the bolder, and the pencil much sharper and more immediately striking than the ink which had faded to a pale silver. I know now that Imelda Dooley, my grandmother, was sixteen when *A Spoiled Priest* was given her by Dorothy Fenely, her school friend at the Dominican Convent, West Maitland. By the time Imelda had a daughter, Dorothy was merely a name, someone the daughter never met. Nor did she ever hear her mother called Till.

I look at the book now, and I see that the red cloth is frayed and faded, and that the spine is skewed so that the leading edges of the boards are no longer aligned — the tell-tale signs of use. Surprising as it might be, *A Spoiled Priest* was not only what one young Australian girl might give another in the years just after Federation, but it was read as well. Perhaps Canon Sheehan was not far wrong, in his general tenor, when on page three he referred to "that shy, half-affectionate, half-reverential manner in which Irish girls are wont to speak of candidates for the priesthood". Murrurundi girls as well.

Canon Sheehan, the parish priest of Doneraile in County Cork, was a prolific and popular writer. *A Spoiled Priest* represents his one advertence to Australia. A footnote to the fifth story "Remanded" says: "This story, founded on fact (the hero-priest is buried in Doneraile), was appropriately printed in Australia at the time of certain sensational accusations publicly brought against a priest by an unhappy woman." Sheehan's good priest is falsely accused by a young female parishioner. She cannot go through with her perjury, and throws herself into a canal. Her intended victim coffins her himself and has her buried, in consecrated ground, to the sullen resentment of his other parishioners. Some days later her disinterred, decomposing body is found beside the bed of the judge who had been hearing her charge. He is "lying on the white coverlet, his head shattered into an indistinguishable mass of bone and blood, his brains blackening the white wall behind his pillow, his right hand clutching a heavy pistol".

The Coningham case in Sydney, for which Canon Sheehan had his story printed, was not lurid tragedy, nor even lurid melodrama. The Very Reverend Denis O'Haran was cited as co-respondent in divorce proceedings brought by Arthur Coningham, a former, if not especially glorious, Test cricketer. It was alleged the adultery took place in the grounds of St Mary's Cathedral. Witnesses were suborned, the posts interfered with, false information fed through spies. The case came to court in the first days of 1901. Federation was a stuffy backdrop, easily ignored as the Coningham farce got cracking. Convents throughout the country stormed heaven. At the Convent of Mercy, Murrurundi, Miss Imelda Dooley said prayers for a special intention. Denis O'Haran, certainly a vain man, was acquitted, and lies now in one of the more lavish graves in Waverley Cemetery.

It was not a Canon Sheehan style of tragedy. "Irish priests are fatalists," he had written, "they are so habituated to the drama of relentless iniquity that is always going on around them — the striking of the feeble with the mailed hand, the chaining of the captive to the victim's car, the sleek, hypocritical but unbending despotism, under which the helpless victims hopelessly writhe; the utter despair of all, as destiny for ever mockingly destroys them, — all these things make the Irish priest patient under circumstances that ordinarily drive men to madness."

Australia however had not allowed the Irish priest such an epic vision. In the new land Canon Sheehan's story had had to be reworked.

When I was a child it was the illustrations to *A Spoiled Priest* that caught my attention. Seven of them include children. But beyond that there was something odd about them. The book holds out great promise to someone leafing through these pictures. There are five plates in the first five pages, another four over the next hundred pages, and then no more for the rest of the book — half the total pagination. Why such plenitude and vigour at the beginning, such pinched meanness for the long stretch after that?

Five of the illustrations feature a priest. In "A Thorough Gentleman" three spivs, but one of them a priest, round off dinner in a hotel dining room with cigars. In "Rita, the Street Singer" the priest (another gentleman — he has lace curtains and bobble-fringed blinds) leans over the waif, and then, in the next picture, he leans over both the waif and her terminally consumptive sister.

"A Spoiled Priest", the first story in the book, has exultant illustrations. Facing the second page, small boys in a jammed barn of a classroom erupt in cheers, toss their caps and satchels in the air, knock over their ink bottles, vault across the desks. By the time they face page three, they are tidier and more orderly, waving their caps — one with even an expression of adoration, his fists clasped together under his chin in grateful supplication — as they flank a priest, a strong figure of a man of about forty, advancing straight through the picture in bowler, frock coat and cape. By the time this priest is facing page four, his hat is in his left hand, as is a cane, and his right hand is on a very small boy's curly head as he says, "And this little fellow must come too". Against page five he is again hatted and on the move, the boy in his arms, smiling. Then the pictures of him cease.

I was able to read when I took down *A Spoiled Priest* from my grandmother's shelf, but I was only about seven, and I was not impelled to go past the pictures. Most of the initial letters for the words in the captions were capitalised, and I wondered over the new, rare adjective in the final picture of the boy enfolded by the priest. "He Wrapped Him Round with the Folds of His Great Maynooth Cloak." I never came across the word in my dictionary. Yet the knowledge of its existence was a bright token of a place for me in another world.

I was both dulled and left uneasy by the title *A Spoiled Priest*. I was seven. The word priest I certainly understood. Priests were real enough. What I could not understand was how a priest could be spoiled. Children were spoiled. To be spoiled was a bad thing. Whereas priests were good.

I turned the illustrations again. One after another, what they showed was a priest blessing and making life happy for young people. The frontispiece was different. It was perhaps grotesque, certainly unnerving. A row of men sat on straightbacked chairs beside one another. Behind, in front, and beyond them, but blurred, were other men. At the end of the row, nearest the surface of the picture, was a large-featured man. The illustration was done in black pen and ink, but with a strong effect of wash. This man wore a long shapeless gown, so generous in its extent that as he sat it hung on him like classical drapery. M. Healy, the illustrator, had spread the wash of the pen, so that the material began to look like weeds, and the weeds from this central figure climbed across the seat beside him which otherwise was empty. His head was bent forward, his bony, high-bridged nose starting to sag into monstrous misshapenness, his eyes closed, his hands slack and sliding into the black and white streaks of the weeds. The caption read: "His Face Was Ashen, His Hands Were Cold and Trembling".

When, at the age of seventeen, I told my father, by letter, that I wanted to become a priest, he came to visit me, in person, at boarding school. It was late on a warm October morning, in the middle of the week; he had taken time out from a heavy schedule. I was called out of class to see him, and we sat side by side on the wooden benches in front of the First Division Building, looking down across the cricket pitch of Third Field West to the handball courts.

"You have made us all very happy," he said. "Your mother and your grandmother have prayed for this since you were a little boy."

I sort of knew this. I said nothing.

"You're sure?" he asked me.

"Yes, I'm quite sure."

"I only ask because I want you to be sure. You need to be sure."

"I know I'm sure."

"I only say this because once you're in, the worst thing that can happen to you is to come out. The most wonderful calling all right is to be a priest, but the worst thing that can happen to a man is to start out and then give it away. I've seen them. Your grandfather will tell you the same thing. Pathetic cases."

"No," I said, "I'm sure."

A Spoiled Priest appeared in the dawn of the great age of the Irish short story. George Moore's *The Untilled Field* preceded it, from the same publisher, in 1903, just two years earlier. "The clergy," says Moore, "are swallowing up the country." Yet he can be more relaxed than that. His Father MacTurnan, for example, a simple, compassionate man, grieves that the only Irish people wealthy enough to marry are the priests, while the rest of the population haemorrhages away to America. He writes to Rome asking that priestly celibacy be revoked. His bishop, tactfully, ignores the eccentricity. Instead he gives Father MacTurnan five pounds so that he can buy a pig for one of his parishioners who has no other way of winning a bride.

The classic Irish short story collection, *Dubliners*, was largely written by 1905. It opens with the words: "There was no hope for him this time: it was the third stroke." Joyce had no need to say that his subject was a priest. His priest is paralysed and mad. Yet the boy narrator believes he owes the priest much.

I did not read *A Spoiled Priest* until I was in my late twenties and my grandmother was dead. I had not got things quite right as a child. Perhaps M. Healy, the illustrator, was to blame. A character, Rita, for example, was depicted as a child of five, but the text told me she was "any age between eight and fourteen". And the mature, broad-shouldered, tortured priest of the frontispiece was not a priest at all. He was a youth, a seminarian, still in his early twenties. On the first page the title story is asterisked, and the footnote is as long as the body of the text itself. In a most delicately toned statement Canon Sheehan explains his title: "This is the term used in some parts of the country to express the failure of a student who has just put his foot within the precincts of the sanctuary, and been rejected. Up to quite a recent period such an ill-fated youth was regarded by the peasantry with a certain amount of scorn, not unmingled with superstition. Happily, larger ideas are being developed even on this subject; and not many now believe that no good fortune can ever be the lot of him who has made the gravest initial mistake of his life."

When I was older I noticed that my grandmother also read John Galsworthy, Frances Parkinson Keyes, M. Barnard Eldershaw, Kate O'Brien.

She never missed writing to me at Easter, blue-black ink in a confident hand. She always ended her letters with the wish: "May the Risen Lord bring you all the joy of the Resurrection morn."

The first time that I brought a girl home to meet her after I left the Society of Jesus, my grandmother was not only courteous, but even welcoming. Cushioned in her invalid's armchair, waited on by my mother, she detailed how a little glass of port wine was very medicinal.

"Is it your preferred drink?" asked the girl.

"At luncheon," said my grandmother. "It goes very nicely with a little broth. But for my dinner I always take a drop of stout."

The girl wrinkled her nose in a friendly fashion.

My grandmother let fly a small, elderly laugh. "It's most nutritious. Ensures a little flesh."

The girl was slim.

Later my grandmother said to me: "And very nice too. Of course you don't have to marry the first one you fall for."

Scattered Leaves

A Biography for Michael Scott

In 1967 Clifton Pugh painted his friend, Father Michael Scott.
Michael Scott was not a famous man. Born in 1910, educated at
Riverview in Sydney, he had entered the Jesuits at seventeen,
and been sent for his studies to Dublin, Innsbruck and Oxford-
shire. He was best known as a champion of the place of contemporary art in the religious life of Australia and a founder of the
Blake Prize. Pugh wanted to paint him. It was a tradition,
although not always honoured, that Rectors of Newman College
should have their portraits painted. Michael Scott's predecessors and successors sit flat on their commissioned canvases,
buoyed by their billowing academic robes. Michael Scott was
painted privately, with no mark of rank or office on him, except
his priestly one, and that because it was one of the tensions of
the personality that Pugh saw in his friend. Michael Scott sits in
a doorway, framed, even cramped, by a vaulted stained glass
arch of scarlet and ochre and aquamarine. The wispy hairs on
the crown of his head reach towards the sea green of a fanlight.
He wears his full black clericals. There is no striking dignity or
even presence about his pose. It appears makeshift, as though
he were told to find himself a seat and wait there while the artist
got on with his work. He faces full on, and is painted to his shins,
and his knees would be at the lower forefront of the portrait if
they were not covered by his clasped hands. Yet the hands are
not fully clasped. They are coming apart. They are unsure,
tentative, provisional, the ring fingers are only just crossed and

the little fingers not touching at all. The legs are clamped together at the knees, then splayed. This is not a male whose natural seated position is the out-flung thighs. The contours and the rhythm of his torso are impenetrable beneath the unrelieved black. So all the more attention is thrown on to his face. It is both avian, and then pixieish in the pointed ears and the tuft of hair in the centre of the bare skull. He gazes out directly at the viewer, but his head is bent to the right and the look he gives is both unsure and whimsical. There is a smile but it is coming from a long way back, through the unstable lenses of his glasses. They have so many angles of refraction that they are more properly seen as being shattered, and the smile, the whimsy, the shyness, the question, the nervousness are all bent and broken by them and flung out, piecemeal and incoherent.

Ten years after Michael Scott left Australia a friend purchased the portrait from Pugh and presented it to Newman College. It hangs in the dining room, to the immediate but recessed left of the High Table, shrinking from the commanding, magisterial eyes of Pugh's inferior Mannix and just in sight of the gentle splendour of a print of Millais's Newman.

In the December 1967 issue of *Twentieth Century* Michael Scott had an article entitled "The Vocation of the Artist". It was a declaration of position, even a manifesto. He wrote of a small group in Australia in the early 1950s trying to encourage religious art, and "learning how futile it was to expect interest, let alone leadership from the Church, either here or in Rome". In the next sentence he suddenly countered himself. "Yet it was from the Church, indeed from Rome itself, in the person of the late Pope Pius XII, that the lead came in an address to a group of Italian artists in April 1952."

Michael Scott cited many thinkers, Clive Bell, Jacques Maritain, Eric Newton, Eric Gill, Christopher Dawson, Baudelaire, and he reconciled their views with statements of Pius XII. Finally he summed up in, he said, his own words.

> Because God knows that as his children, even the pale reflections of himself that we are, we too have in us our own seeds of creativeness, he deliberately leaves a good deal of the beauty of his creation obscure, covering it over with a veil of distracting and confusing detail and even seeming ugliness, so that we might ourselves have the joy of discovering the essential beauty beneath. And to help us in this search for hidden beauty, somehow, in his own mysterious way, he implants in each one of us the prototypes of that beauty, so that we shall recognize it when the time comes.

Fisher Library at the University of Sydney once had a standing order for every work of fiction published in the United Kingdom. In 1972 I went there as a postgraduate student in twentieth century Anglo–Irish literature. I took from the shelves in stack Mary Lavin's books, the first time I had ever seen them. As I stood in the bay, the first "story" that caught my eye in the volumes I touched, the recent works of her maturity, was the one told by the dedications. *The Great Wave* of 1961 was dedicated "To M.S." Her next volume, *In the Middle of the Fields* (1967) was "To Michael Scott S.J." Her next book came out in 1969, the year she and Michael Scott were married. It was called *Happiness* and was dedicated to two of her daughters. I moved over into the natural light of the embrasured window and read the title story. I was thrown, then I was laughing, at the technical cheekiness of it. The narrator is the eldest of three daughters of a widow. The male presence in their family life is a priest. He is taken for granted as belonging, and he comes and goes as any other member of the household. The story's focus, however, is the widow, or more accurately mother, her exuberant and manic life, and her running commentary on the notion of happiness. It is only when she collapses out in the twilight garden that the daughters see in the panicked movements of the priest the voice and step of a lover. "Effortlessly he picked her up to carry her into the house."

I stared down at the students mooching to and from the library. I was shocked, I was embarrassed at the give-away intimacy of this story. To say she was betraying Michael Scott wasn't correct. To describe it as exposing him would be too strong as well. Yet the duration and the degree of the intimacy that she described, or perhaps imagined, or even wished had been, should it have been so spelt out? Oh, theirs was a great love story, and there was nothing indecorous in "Happiness", but attractive as this priest was, his devotion to one family and his barely understood love for the widow were … were what? I gazed, unseeing, through the double glazing, and the students came and went. What was dedication? Could one vow displace an earlier, and no dark shadow fall like a question across both loyalties?

Yet none of this was the subject of "Happiness". In fact the story was hardly about the priest. For all his lifting the widow across the threshold he was pushed aside at the deathbed. It was mother and daughters who understood and carried one another. Then I found myself grieving for the priest excluded at the end.

The widow in "Happiness" is named Vera, the true woman. In other stories of Mary Lavin's maturity, there was a widow, and she was named Vera.

In 1992 Mary Lavin spoke on a Radio Telefis Eireann documentary. She was asked little about her work or her daughters. Family and literary friends did that. She was asked about Michael Scott, and the thirty-five years of their correspondence after they met as students at University College Dublin in 1934, and about the handful of meetings during his years as a Jesuit.

"Were you at ease with him?" she was asked.

"At ease!" she laughed. "We were really married."

The interviewer prompted her to finish the story.

"He rang me up one night and he said, "Mary, I'm leaving," and he said, "I'm coming," and he came. And I think I remember sort of half-resenting it. Ooh, I'd had a whale of a time as a widow."

Michael Scott's two closest Jesuit friends were with him when he was presented with the documents that would release him from the Society of Jesus. All three were in tears. It took the presence of their Provincial, Peter Kelly, to steady them. Only then could Michael Scott step forward and sign the papers. Soon after, before he left Melbourne to start his new life with Mary Lavin, he destroyed all her letters to him.

The Sidney Nolan Retrospective in Dublin in 1973 was the largest that had been held anywhere in the world. It was opened on 18 June at the RDS in Ballsbridge by Lord Clark in the presence of the *Taoiseach*. Every Australian registered with the Embassy as being resident in Ireland was invited. I recognised the faces of the Embassy secretaries. Otherwise I knew no one. Blessedly there were the paintings one could look at. I could go home. While at university I had eaten three times a day under the hall-long curve of *River Bend*. The tiling of *Desert Flowers* across the wall spread an Australian light over everyone there. I stepped back and looked around to see the reaction to this, and I saw Michael Scott. He stood apart but not altogether by himself. From the photographs on her books I recognised his wife. She was ahead of him, on the edge of a crowd, talking and animated. Michael Scott stared distractedly, intently, on the lookout for someone, but he had the air of a man for whom this stance was a ploy to avoid taking part in something where he does not feel quite at home.

I hesitated. I did not know how he regarded any association with his former life. I had never been in his presence as an equal, as an independent adult. I had never addressed him as anything other than "Father", and I could not do that here. I went over to him.

"Michael Scott?" I said.

"Yes," he said, and concentrated on me.

"Gerry Windsor."

"Oh, Threepence." He leant back and smiled and twitched the frames of his glasses. "And what are you doing here?"

I went home and recorded what he had to say to me.

He loved Bective, he had said, Mary's farm in County Meath. But they had to live most of the time in Mary's mews in Dublin because Mary's youngest daughter, Caroline, was still in her last year at university.

Twenty years later, on 16 June 1993, I walked across south Dublin from Sandymount to the *Irish Times* office in D'Olier Street where Mary's youngest daughter, Caroline, was the Features Editor.

"Mick," she said when I explained myself, "my stepfather, my beloved stepfather."

He could see himself retiring to Bective, he told me, and being very happy there. The previous year, for the first time since Mary's first husband had died, they had pastured the one hundred acres, and had got £2,000 for the cattle. If he were there fulltime, he was sure he could get £3,000 the next year.

"Mother sold Bective," Caroline said in 1993. "She just got it into her head. She talked to no one. Not even Mick. She just went ahead. I don't know why. It was probably a pity."

He hated the city, he told me. I wondered whether he liked Ireland all that much. He was certainly lucky, he said, to get his job, especially when he was sixty-three. In Ireland particularly. You had no chance at all unless you knew people. The place was ridden with that sort of thing.

"When he died," Caroline reported to me, "Mick was just another elderly parishioner to the parish priest. Didn't really know him. It was to be just a quiet ordinary funeral. Mother was very unwell, my eldest sister was just out of hospital after major surgery, the family was all upset, and it was those lost days between Christmas and New Year. I was in the porch, about to go in, and this taxi drew up. Out jumped Frank Martin, the Augustinian, the historian, with vestments over his arm. "I just saw it in the paper. I rushed over. I have to take part in the Mass." I was about to go in again, and there was another priest, running. "I've been sent by the Jesuit Provincial," he said. "I'd like to be a celebrant at the Mass." They all spoke, everyone spoke. The Jesuit said that Mick had come, late, to make his home in Ireland and he had been loved by all who knew him. But long before that, this Jesuit said, Mick had been a cherished member of another family, the Society of Jesus, and he had never really ceased to belong to that family. That was when the tears really came to my eyes."

He hadn't been home, he told me in 1973, since he left Australia five years previously. Mary refused to fly. They were going to spend the summer holidays in Normandy. Mary liked France, and he would tour the D Day battlefields.

"I went with them," Caroline remembered. "It wasn't the only time. When I was a child at school I was going with them. Mick spent his time combing the battlefields and the war cemeteries all over Europe. He was looking for his brother Tony. He'd been an airman. Mick couldn't get Tony out of his head. In the last few years of his life he wrote a book, well a sort of book, about Tony. A lot of it about types of planes and so forth. We promised we'd get it bound up for him, a number of copies. He loved Tony, Tony was his youngest brother, and because the parents both died when he was quite young, he always felt a special responsibility for Tony. Mick said that when Tony went out on a mission, he would make sure he always flew over the college where Mick was studying, in Oxford I think it was. And when they came back too. But then he didn't come back. Mick was obsessed with finding out what happened to him. He tramped everywhere in Europe, living in hope of finding Tony — his plane, his body even, maybe his grave. Mother and I went with him."

"It's very stimulating," Michael Scott said to me, "living with a writer. Full of nervous energy."

"You must understand," Caroline told me, "Mother had a very difficult ageing."

Father Charles Fraser was in the front garden at Riverview. He wore a floppy white hat and long grey slacks and canvas gauntlets that covered his arms to the elbows. The secateurs clicked sharply and with regularity as he moved through the beds of bare rose stems. He caught the futile growths as they were snapped free and tossed them behind him on to the tarred path. The thorny trail led all around the garden.

Charlie Fraser was alone, the only figure between the long massive pile of Hawkesbury sandstone and the precipitous overgrown slope to the river. Around him the paths radiated through the firm lawn.

A man emerged from upstage on the level turning circle around the statue of the Sacred Heart, and stood at the top of the steps that descended to the garden. He moved directly but with no great confidence towards the pruner. Charlie Fraser was aware of him, but he neither looked up nor paused. He was used to strangers arriving at the front of the school, finding him the only person about and wanting directions. He let them come to him. All the way. He would not have the rhythm or concentration of his work disturbed. The man approached, his walk still unsure. He had come out too far now either to go back or stop, stranded. He strengthened his stride and came up with the gardener, just the scattering of lopped twigs between them. Only then did Charlie Fraser begin, stiffly, to turn his body around.

"Hello, Charlie," said the man.

Charlie Fraser was taken aback, but his natural dry reserve combined with his stiffness and he showed no reaction. He looked the man in the face. It must be an old boy, he thought. A very old old boy, a contemporary of his own. Almost no one addressed him by his name. "Hello," he said, with a hint of question, a hint of distancing in his voice.

"You don't recognise me?" said the man.

"No. I don't," said Charlie with a sharp, almost indifferent honesty.

"It's Mick," said the man, not moving forward.

Charlie Fraser shielded his eyes and stared at the thin seamed face.

"Oh my God, Mick, so it is," he said. He hoisted his rear leg and yanked it around so that he stood evenly facing the man. He smiled, and it could have been amusement at his own slowness, and he nodded his head gently. He closed and fastened the secateurs and clamped them under his arm. Then he drew off the long gauntlets and dropped them on the path in front of him. He raised his foot carefully to step out of the bed. Mick put his hand out to steady him. "Thank you, I'm okay," said Charlie.

Charlie Fraser was a cousin of Michael Scott and a few years behind him as a boy at Riverview. As a priest Charlie Fraser taught me Classics, sometimes just the pair of us, and for hours each day.

"I lived there with Mick at Campion Hall, that Junior school," he told me, "helping him get the place ready before it opened. In 1946 or whenever it was. I remember one night. We were sitting around the fire. It must have been winter. Lou Lachal —

who got swallowed up by that mission in India — he was there too. Mick had this old dog, Brownie it was called, and in it came with this black hat in its mouth. It dropped the hat on the floor and sat a few inches behind it and barked at us and cuffed the hat a few times, the way dogs do. We sat there amused. Then suddenly I realised and I said, "That might be my hat," so I got up and went out to the hallway, and my hat was still there okay. Lou Lachal stopped laughing. "Good heavens, it might be my hat," he said, and he got up and went out to have a look. Sure enough it was his hat that the dog had. Next morning Lou went into town to David Jones and bought himself a black Borsellino velour hat, the best in the shop, and sent the bill to Mick Scott."

"Brownie was devoted to him," I said. "Went everywhere with him."

"Oh, he was a wonderful fellow, Mick. I really loved him," he said.

Michael Scott only revisited Australia once after he left it, and the Society of Jesus, in 1968. On that occasion, in 1982, he drove up to Riverview. He met only one person, he related back in Ireland, and he got the feeling that he wasn't welcome. So he took it no further, didn't go inside, and never went back there.

He wrote to a friend in Melbourne for twenty-one years. He had no regrets, he said, either for his forty years as a Jesuit or for the new step he had taken.

He told his friend that he had started on his book about Tony in 1977, on his retirement. He wrote 100,000 words. He said it contained the fullest account yet of the Bremen raid. He had a foreword written to it by Hughie Edwards V.C. In October 1981 he said it was finished. He said he wanted to write an account now of his childhood at Morisset on the shores of Lake Macquarie. It was an incredibly happy childhood, and he wanted to recall and record it. His father was the Medical Superintendent of the Mental Hospital there, and those four years, 1914 to 1918, were the most wonderful time for a boy. He wanted to revisit Australia and go to Morisset. He came when he was 72. He had not thought he would live so long. His mother had died when she was 46, his father when he was 50. He had a great time in Australia and recovered something of what he had lost in fifteen years in Ireland — a sense of being an Australian.

Rigby in Australia rejected his book about Tony, saying it was well written and well researched, but dull as dishwater. He went to work trying to smarten it up for another try elsewhere. He had the energy now because Mary was more back to her old form. He thought constantly of his wonderful visit home in '82 and longed to go again. He went to the Keppoch country in Scotland and found the tombstone of his maternal, MacDonald, great-great-grandfather. He went again and although he still had a fair bit to find out it was all adding up. Mary's youngest granddaughter, just turning two, was the joy of his life. Instead of calling him Granddad she called him Dadgran. In the summer he had six months at Bective, the longest for five or six years, and he loved being there and the work in the garden restored him and he was ready to go back to the Dublin apartment and resume work on the family history. Mary was her old self again. If she stayed that way he wanted to come out to Australia for two months but it also depended on his angina. He knew he was well into injury time and was crossing his fingers that the whistle wouldn't blow for a little while yet.

He fell and broke his hip. The long-deferred decision to sell Bective hit them both hard. He postponed his trip to Australia till the following year. At least they got a reasonable price for Bective and expected to be able to live on the income. It couldn't be for too long. Their troubles were mainly over. Mary was the best she had been for a long time, and if her health kept up he would be out to Australia for two months. It was, needless to say, very much on his mind. They had had a few more ups and downs, all the inevitable accompaniments of old age. A suspect growth on his neck, a hernia, arthritis. He hesitated to leave Mary alone. That's why he kept postponing the trip. But he wanted so much to come. He missed Bective badly, but he was lucky that his years as a J. had taught him to let go when the time came and not look back too much. He was sorry his inactive life made him boring and his letters short. He promised to try to do better when he saw the light appearing again at the end of that tunnel.

He had an excuse for not writing, he had joined the club by having a coronary. The doctor said OK about flying to Australia but as it would soon be winter there he would wait till August. When he thought about what a wonderful, full rich life he had had, he could scarcely complain about occasional setbacks in his 80th year. He had a cataract operation imminent and Mary was up and down so he was making no firm booking, but the trip was theoretically on for September–October. He was grateful for the concern about his operation. The first thing the surgeon said to him when he came to was that he had taken out the whole of his stomach but left all his bowel. Regaining his strength was a slower matter than he had expected. Walking to the bathroom one night without his stick, he had had a fall and gave himself a nasty hernia near the groin. But the G.P. said he wouldn't let him have another operation and he must put up with it. Many people had them for twenty years or more. He sent his love.

Mick died in Christmas week 1990. Two days before, when Mary's son-in-law arrived at the apartment to tell Mick he must go to hospital, the place was in darkness. Desmond hesitated before the bell, then gently let himself in with his own key. Inside he leant both hands against the door and eased it shut. There was neither light nor sound anywhere in the apartment. But he knew they were there somewhere. He didn't want to disturb, but he had come to disturb. "Mick," he called softly into the dark. He stood still and waited. "Mick," he called again, but it was no louder than before, and the click of the name faded, unanswered, in the gloom. He turned and switched on the light inside the front door, and walked forward into the living room. There was no one there, or in the kitchen, but a smell of cooking lingered and there were newly washed dishes drying by the sink and the tray reset for Mary's breakfast sat on the bench. He called again, "Mick, Mary". He felt the tight membrane of the silence, the barely repressed indrawn breath of children. He was loath to go into the bedroom. He was not being welcomed and they had a right to sanctuary. Yet his purpose could not be deflected. He moved apologetically to the open bedroom door. He did not look in but he positioned himself so that the greater mass of darkness would overshadow the couple inside. Still they did not respond to him. He stood at the door and tapped, and called the two names again, and stepped in. His eyes had no trouble, there seemed to be no gloom. He saw Mick and Mary lying together on their backs, under the coverlet, their hands clasped and resting on Mick's stomach, and Mick's other hand warming and polishing, in benediction, on the knot of their fingers.

"Mick," said Desmond as gently as he could and even as he withdrew, "I'll be back in the morning. It's time for you to leave. They'll be waiting. You must come just as you are."

I saw Michael Scott on only one occasion after 1973. It was 15 October 1988, on the site of my old primary school, Campion Hall, at Point Piper in Sydney. Michael Scott had left Campion Hall in 1952 after the decision was taken to close it. He had suggested the foundation and been its first headmaster, and the task of winding it up was given to another, Father John Farmer. In 1988 old boys were invited to a reunion, with dinner in the old art room, Mass in what had been a courtyard. Father Farmer said the Mass. Deceased old boys were named and prayed for.

They included an exact contemporary of mine, a small freckled larrikin whom I shall call Paul Kinsella. In a mock trial at the age of seven I had been defence counsel for Paul Kinsella, the defendant, when he was charged with wantonly killing a seagull. It was alleged that he had been throwing stones on the waterfront at Rose Bay and a bird had been hit. It had been further alleged that he had deliberately aimed to kill the bird. Paul Kinsella's diminutive mischievous look, his high, quickfire rasp of a voice, his sharp, undeniably furtive movements made his defence an uphill battle. I have no memory of the trick, no notion of the twist of the evidence, but he was acquitted.

After Mass there were pre-dinner drinks. Patrick Kinsella, Paul's older brother, was there. He was now a rogue barrister. He took exclusively criminal work, and he was the object of a constant stream of warnings and admonitions from the bench. He stood talking to a contemporary of his own, Jeremy Flynn, a priest, and one popularly regarded as mad.

I joined them. There was a lull as they acknowledged my presence. "I just wanted to say," I said to Patrick, "how sorry I was to hear about Paul. I'd no idea he'd died. How long ago was it?"

"Oh, five or six years now," said Patrick evenly, waving his hand. "Suddenly."

There was a brief pause.

"In the act of coition," said Jeremy Flynn. He gazed, abstracted, towards my waist. "In the arms of his mistress," he added.

I stared at him. His face was blank, impenetrable. I turned to Patrick.

"It's perfectly true," he said. There was a trace of a smile there, no trace of grief.

After the main course had been cleared away and before the speeches, there was a short video screening. Michael Scott, recorded, spoke to us from Dublin. He had hoped, he said, he had intended, to come for the dinner. He had only happy

memories of Campion Hall, he was inordinately proud of his
boys, he wished them well, he was with them in spirit. He
looked drawn and the heavy frames of his glasses gave a harsh
asymmetry to the lines on his face. The clothes hung starkly from
his upper body. I found it awkward to look at him. It was fifteen
years since I had seen him. It was nearly forty since most of the
other old boys present had done so. He had nothing further to
say. He looked down at us in silence and a little uneasily while
he waited for the camera to stop rolling. The picture went out in
a crackle and there was a blank moment. Then the screen came
alive again. It was a Campion Hall picnic in 1948, recorded as
some parent's home movie. I was not in it. It had happened two
years before I went to school. Boys dotted the large terraced
garden of a home in Vaucluse. None of them was older than ten.
They burst in front of the lens and somersaulted and did hand-
stands and scampered away. They careered along the grassed
levels and unpredictably around corners in flight or pursuit.
They queued and jostled for sausages and tomato sauce. Their
mothers attended and fed and watched them, still points in the
pell-mell life of the hillside garden. At a distance, flanked by the
tiny John Farmer, moved Michael Scott. He was thirty-eight, in
full black clericals, with his hat in his hand. He was apart and
both urbane and austere in his bearing, but the bubbling life
swirled in and eddied around him and raced away again. He
smiled with the mothers, and pointed out of camera and they
all laughed, and the boys swarmed again. I was not there but I
could hear the cries in the garden, and I could hear them echoing
in the hall at Campion as the film was replayed term after term
of my schooldays. I was caught up in the high shouts and the
gleeful recognitions and the cheers of the picnickers, of the
whole school, as they all remembered the occasion or remembered the long arcing joy of it and then remembered nothing but
the soft, spent ease beyond the film.

My Mother's House

When I was a very small boy my mother took me out to Sans
Souci to visit my Auntie Claude. Auntie Claude had been born
in 1856, and in fact she was my mother's mother's aunt. Auntie
Claude's parents had arrived in Sydney from Stirlingshire in
1854 with an infant daughter. But the child died. In 1856 they
had the first of their Australian-born children, and they called
her Rose. When I first met Rose she had been a Sister of Mercy
for over seventy years. By then she was Auntie Claude. All the
girls from the upper Hunter, my mother said, went to school
either to the Josephites at Lochinvar or to the Mercys at Singleton. Rose went to Singleton and then entered the convent there.
So did her younger sister, Margaret. Margaret was my Auntie
Gertrude, but she died in February 1947 and I have no memory
of having met her. Gertrude was a very capable woman, my
mother always maintained, and she went from Singleton to
found the Mercy Convent at Broken Hill.

Sans Souci was another initiative of Auntie Gertrude. My
mother related that Auntie Gertrude wanted a holiday house
for her nuns away from the heat and rigour of Broken Hill, so
in 1939 she built a convent at Sans Souci on a hill overlooking
Kogarah Bay. In time nuns came to live in retirement and die
there, as Auntie Claude did in 1953. After that the relatives of
Sisters Gertrude and Claude never had reason to go to Sans
Souci again. The visits all belonged to another age. "We used
to go there by trolley bus," my mother remembered, and I saw
myself outside a lowering porch, on a narrow strip of crisp

lawn, dodging around yew bushes, and there was the black
shape and the tiny face of a gnarled beetle who was my Auntie
Claude.

I rang my mother when I saw the notice. "Under instructions
from the Sisters of Mercy, Due to the Sale of the Property,
Unreserved Auction of Contents of Chapel and Convent."

"Let's go out," I said to my mother.

"I'll ring first," she decided.

"There's a number for the auctioneer," I told her.

"No, I'll ring the convent."

"I spoke to a Sister Annette," she said later. "She said to be
sure and introduce ourselves to her when we went out."

Twice in the following week my mother spoke to me on the
phone, and asked, "Do you still want to go out to Sans Souci?"

The row of box gums on the footpath had been shorn flat. The
lines of the convent were unobscured.

"I don't remember the second storey," said my mother.

"This looks much newer than 1939," I said. But this was the
convent we had visited. The honey and cream bricks and the
unfussy Romanesque pilasters had not stained or worn or
crumbled. The moat of lawn was there, and the yew bushes,
dark green and conker-filled or lighter green under a yellow
icing, and bare frangipanis and a white poinsettia in flower. This
was a holiday home, on a corner block with a Norfolk Island
pine outside the chapel. The mat at the front door said MERCY.

There were auctioneer's signs and arrows everywhere, most
of them saying, "Please Respect the Sisters' Privacy". We followed the directions, into the refectory. There was a kitchen at
one end, and a group of late middle-aged women were talking
there. My mother stood at the door and asked, "Sister Annette?"

Sister Annette took us into the kitchen and introduced us. We
stood around the great table with the nuns and they gave us
coffee and reintroduced us as others of their sisters came in.

They remembered Auntie Claude, but it was Auntie Gertrude they honoured.

"You'd hardly have known they were sisters."

"Sister Claude was so tiny, with a very deep voice. She'd come into the chapel and say, "What's going on in here?""

"Mother Gertrude was a lovely person, a wonderful conversationalist. So interesting to talk to about anything."

"She could hold her own anywhere. Would've known exactly what to do with the governor."

"When famous singers came to the towns, they'd always put on a special recital just for the nuns. Mother Gertrude would thank them, and she'd do it so gracefully."

"She was a great businesswoman," added my mother. "My mother always used to say that about Auntie Gertrude."

"Is there a history of the congregation?" I asked. "A pamphlet, or a written account just for your own use?"

"No, no. Just what's in the archives at Parkes."

"Do you have many novices?" I asked.

"Oh, people come and go. But we haven't had a profession in twenty years."

I took photos of the nuns and my mother together in the kitchen.

"We mustn't take up any more of your time," my mother said. "If we could just have a look around."

"It's been lovely to meet you," the nuns all said. "It's so good to meet people who remember the old ones."

My mother and I followed all the signs and all the arrows through and outside the house. A low-ceilinged lock-up under the house comprised one complete auction lot — about fifty old suitcases, then crutches, walking frames, commodes, wheelchairs, two walking sticks. "One of these could well have been Auntie Claude's," I suggested.

"Oh come out of there, Gerry," my mother called.

We went upstairs, a circular metal staircase winding up a wall of glass bricks in a round, bright hub of a chamber. In the recreation room my mother pointed to the little internal casement windows that opened over the back of the chapel. "For the elderly and sick nuns who couldn't manage the stairs," she explained to me. "So they could get to Mass."

In the chapel people were speaking at secular volume, strolling unrestricted, lifting, peering, tapping with their knuckles. We went into the sacristy first. Much of the floor was covered by a collection of old oak and pine stools, two-legged, oval in shape, with a small hole in the middle of the seat where the fingers could slip through and grip.

"They'd be good," I said. "Stools are always useful."

My mother checked them against the catalogue, and we muttered and half finished sentences, wondering how to assess such objects. I had no idea what stools were worth. Other items took our attention. Outside the chapel door "a 19th century Wedgwood meat platter 'Ivanhoe Overthrows the Templat'." Beside the holy water font "a carved hall stand and seat". A curiosity I had never seen, "a confessional kneeler", with its detachable piece of slatted board, to shield penitent from confessor.

My mother and I meandered our own ways through brassware and glassware and pews and statues and stacked pictures. We came together at the altar. I opened my mouth to speak and my mother spoke before me. "This is very sad," we both said.

The silver-plated tabernacle doors were just ajar. I opened them. The veil was drawn, but I slid my fingers between the two squares of material and tugged them back along the line of gilt thread. There was nothing inside but the padding. A hollow of quilted satin.

On the way out I saw one of the nuns. "What were those stools in the sacristy used for?" I asked.

"We used to sit on those in the dining room. In the old days."

"Deportment," said my mother. "Straight backs."

"I'll go back tomorrow," I told her.

She rang me at ten in the morning.

"I'm just going out the door, on my way now," I said.

"Sure you really want to? You don't have to."

"I'm going. Now what do you want me to bid on?"

"Well, I'd quite like the meat plate … a stool …"

"The hall stand?"

"Yes."

"What are you willing to go to?"

"Oh I don't know. I'll leave it to you."

"Well, for example, do I go to five hundred on the meat plate?"

"Good heavens no! One hundred. I don't mind if I don't get it."

"The stools?"

"What about forty?"

"OK."

"I'll look after it," said my mother crisply.

The chapel was miniature and so bright. The transepts were only about four metres deep, and there was no stained glass, but open windows around the sanctuary, even behind the altar. The chapel was packed, pews and aisles and floor all jammed. Upstairs in their recreation room the nuns took up position, looking down through their casement windows. I stood at the front of the nave and leaned against the modern table altar. Beside me, on the floor, a man distracted two small boys with Coke and Fanta. I kept getting a whiff of cigarette smoke. Two dealers sat on the altar steps facing the people, in the twin prelatial seats, lots 2 and 3, each "an oak carver chair". The auctioneer took his place on the top altar step, and used a marble ambo as his rostrum.

He repeated a request from the sisters for decorum, he related how after much prayer and consideration they had decided to put matters in the hands of Gray Eisdell Timms, and the firm was very conscious of the honour. Then he spun into action. He was good. He used his patter to establish his credentials.

"Rosemary, would you hold up the cruets. Look at her. Must have been an altar boy. Or learnt it from her two sons who were altar boys at Bexley, now both at St Joseph's College. In fact we have a large Catholic representation at Gray Eisdell Timms. I'm sure no one here's going to hold that against us. I myself went through school first with the sisters, and then under the Christian Brothers at St Virgil's, Hobart. What am I bid for this assortment of Mass cruets?"

He swept on. A large number of Our Ladys came up, each simply "a plaster religious statue of Our Lady". He sold the Queen of Heaven for $320, and Our Lady of Lourdes for $380, and announced a "stone religious statue of Our Lady". The figure was kneeling and her ankles and clogs were showing and she held a pair of Rosary beads. There was some murmuring and craning to see, and confusion in the air, until one of the nuns called from the casement, "It's Saint Bernadette".

Saint Bernadette brought $200 and the rhythm settled itself again. The dealers sat in their carved oak and with a grim nonchalance crushed any opposition for the classier, recyclable items. "The bid is on the altar," cried the auctioneer, and the dealers took all the pews for $570 each, and the marble font for $640, and an oak sick-call box for $280, and a brass credence table with marble top, the only credence table the auctioneer had handled in ten years, for $780, and a pair of five sconce brass candelabra for $220 each. "The bid is on the altar, here beside me on the altar," called the auctioneer again and again.

The dispersal was relentless, and not cheap. The hall stand went for $380, the meat platter for $560, the crib figures for $600 to a "lady", the Stations of the Cross for $600 to a young woman, a past pupil of Loreto, Kirribilli, and her boyfriend, who were going to put them on the walls of their house.

In the whole room there were only two obvious groups of

religious professionals. One man was addressed by the auctioneer as "monsignor", but I thought it probably a trade nickname,
for there were several other dealers on terms of intimacy with
the auctioneer, and "the monsignor" was Middle Eastern and
wore lay clothes and a heavy gold chain around his neck. But he
was a bona fide monsignor all right, a Chaldaean Syrian, and
although he stood he was accompanied by three seated nuns, in
full cream and caramel habits, all Iraqis. Immediately in front of
him were three figures in full black. A slight sandy-haired man
in tailored clericals stood throughout, a fixed half smile on his
face. It broadened just a few degrees when items such as Sacred
Hearts were held up, and he would give a slight, knowing roll
of his eyes to his companions. Beside him was a nun, a hand-
some young woman with black glasses and a severe set to her
mouth. To her right was a stout, curly haired young priest who
wore a European clerical soutane. He had a bidding card stuffed
face down in the sash. For the first eighty items he did not touch
it.

Then the auctioneer announced the centrepiece of the day's
sale, "a magnificently carved marble central altar". The tabernacle was being sold separately, he said. "An altar like this, if
new," he said, "would cost you at least $50,000." He paused and
looked around, and his finger shot out, "One thousand I have".
The dealers on the altar scanned ahead in their catalogues; they
had no interest. It was a two-sided duel, the Chaldaean monsignor and the stout priest in the cassock. They traded blows
evenly.

"Well, it'll be going to a good home," said the auctioneer. The
young priest lolled against the confessional kneeler. Lay seconds, or perhaps backers, even bankrollers, crowded at his
shoulder, whispering. The monsignor kept smiling, but he was
no match. At $5200 he gave in. For the first time the crowd
applauded. The nun beside the young priest, the successful
bidder, was impassive, motionless. Only then I noticed the
medallion on her chest — in copper relief, the profile of Saint

Pius X. Ah, I realised, these were Archbishop Lefebvre's break-away lot, the Catholics more Catholic than the Pope.

"We'll do the side altars separately," said the auctioneer. "The successful bidder has the option of taking the second at the same price. I should point out that in case the purchaser is not a religious body, the relics in the altar will have to be removed."

The monsignor was unopposed. He took both altars for $650 apiece. The auctioneer was clearly relieved. "No need now for the relics to be taken out." He made another speech about the need for the separate purchasers of the main altar and the tabernacle to co-operate on the removal of the one from the other. But the cassocked priest got the tabernacle too, for $720. Again the crowd clapped.

When the auctioneer came to item 91, "a brass monstrance and case", he pointed out a delicate matter. "There is a further piece to the monstrance which the sisters have withheld. Again, if the purchaser is a religious body, they will hand over the piece. If not they will retain it. So the item you are now bidding for is the monstrance as is." The glass frame that had actually touched the Host could not go to just anybody.

The Chaldaean and the plump priest in the cassock competed again. The monsignor ran his opponent up hard. The monstrance reached $1550 before it went to the breakaway Catholics. The applause was sustained.

"Congratulations," said the auctioneer, "the most popular bidder in the room". I wondered if there was any question whether the sisters would be handing over the missing piece to a schismatic body.

The schismatics and their entourage left. We were running down towards the assortments of "sundry bric-a-brac" and "sundry religious prints etc", and I had nothing. My resolve hardened towards the stools. I wasn't going to let go of Auntie Claude and Auntie Gertrude. We reached lot 121, the first stool. The option rule applied to all ten stools, said the auc-tioneer. The successful bidder could take either all or only as many as desired. The bidding opened slowly, at twenty, but a young woman on the altar steps beat me up. She pulled out at seventy. But new blood came rushing in down the back.

"Eighty," the auctioneer called.

I nodded.

"Ninety."

His hand jabbed towards the back. "One hundred."

I couldn't go on past a hundred. Forty, my mother had said. I shook my head. The hammer fell. "How many?" called the auctioneer.

"All of them," I heard her call.

The disappointment pummelled me.

"So, lots 121 to 130 at $100 each," said the auctioneer, annotating his sheets.

There was a flurry at the back. One of the assistants called out, "The lady thought it was $100 for the lot."

The auctioneer gave a genial smile. "I'll put them up again," he said, and began to scratch out in his sheets.

My resolve turned to iron. We would, we would sit down with Auntie Claude and Auntie Gertrude. They would stay with us, and we with them at whatever poor meal or feast there was. I nodded ruthlessly till there was no opposition.

"How many would you like?" asked the auctioneer.

"Five," I said. My mother had five sons. Dimly I remembered the mother's voice asking, "Shall my sons sit with you, on either side?"

"Would you like to choose them?" asked the auctioneer.

"Could I make that six," I called.

The auctioneer nodded and scratched out, rearranging, redistributing the stools.

"I'm so glad," said one of the nuns. "They would have been here at the beginning."

A summer squall hit me as I drove away. Straight ahead, on the horizon beyond the end of Rocky Point Road, silver lightning jagged itself out as sharply as Constantine's cross. The wipers raced. The dry summer leaves whirled in the torrential rain. I could not get home quickly enough to drive with my wife and my son to my mother's house and to have each one of us carry in the stools, two by two, and set them before her.

The Blood of Christ

Father and son, we sit in the frontmost occupied pew at Saint Michael's, Stanmore, Sunday after Sunday, and together we try to get, and keep, a grip on things.

We both have our problems. Harry's eyes have trailed about the iconography, all the statuary dating from the opening of the church in 1910. Neither Saint Francis Xavier nor the Little Flower have held his attention. The patronal figure, Saint Michael, has been more interesting, and I have not had to explain anything. The archangel is in the ascendent over the pint-sized dragon, but most of the rounds are still to go. Just within the last week some power has torn away Michael's left arm and broken off his sword at the hilt. The struggle is poised. Beside it Saint Joseph refuses to look. He gazes down on us, restful, the Christ Child in his arms.

"Who's that?" Harry has asked me when he is five.

I am reciting the Creed. I have to make a quick theological elision. "That's Joseph, Jesus's Dad."

Our pew is beside the alcove where the Sacred Heart holds out his arms. Harry scrutinises this ringleted, bearded figure, then throws a glance back at Joseph high on his entablature. "Yes," he confirms, "he looks like Jesus."

I know this empirical approach is mined with pitfalls. When he is six Harry has taken in the details of the Consecration. Father John Ford holds up the wafer and announces, "Take and eat. This is my body. Do this in memory of me."

Harry, dangling over the kneeler, swings his face to me. The incredulity is transparent, the disgust just showing. "Body!" he explodes, and the gentle detonation reverberates out amongst the faithful.

The questions brim. Sermons are just an occasion for our imaginations to be scratched into play. I am hearing Luke's story of the Sadducees with their riddle about the final heavenly status of the woman married seven times. I register the hypocrisy of the Sadducees because they had no belief in the resurrection in any case. Most of all I am seized by the implication of Christ's answer. "Those judged worthy to attain to the resurrection from the dead will neither marry nor be given in marriage, for they cannot die any more." So, we marry because we are going to die? I wonder whether I have ever properly read this text before.

"And Dad," Harry leans in abruptly and whispers, "what happened to the woman who looked back?"

"Ssh. What? What do you mean?"

"You know, last night, in the story, when everything was being destroyed."

"What? Ohh, Lot's wife. Tell you later."

"But what happened?"

"She was turned into a pillar of salt."

"Yes, but after that?"

"I don't know. We're not told. She was preserved I suppose."

"Does God usually destroy things?"

"Well ... not if they're worth keeping. I think. I hope."

"Is God true?"

"Yes. But I hardly know the first thing about him. Ssh. Now listen to Father."

We bob up together, flurried, caught by the sermon's ending, and we recite the Nicene Creed.

The age of seven, according to the tradition I follow, is the age of reason. That seems to mean the questions tail away then, or at least they are not aired. It is the time children are thought ready for Communion. But when Harry turns seven, my wife, an Anglican, steps in.

"He can't possibly make it. He's never even heard of the Pope."

"Well …" I shrug.

We slog on, into the prayers and the first hanging loops of the mystery, and Harry is nine by the time we get there.

He comes back alone, from the altar. "It's all right," he tells me. "It doesn't really taste like bread."

"No, it's different."

"Now can I have the drink too?"

"No, wait for a while. You're not used to that."

"Is it good?"

"A bit … sticky."

"I don't mind."

"No, take a leaf out of Jesus's book. 'Let this chalice pass me by,' he said to his father."

"Ohh Dad."

"No."

Later, we are together in our front pew. It is Communion time, and there is no one to distribute the chalice. By now it is Father John Milliken who presides, and he raises his eyebrow at me. I go forward.

"The Body of Christ," he says to me.

"Amen," I answer. I take the wafer and consume it.

"The Blood of Christ."

"Amen."

I clasp the chalice, and take just the slightest sip of what could be called a sweet, distasteful ichor. Then I stand beside John Milliken, and I hold the chalice ready to offer it to other men and women. It is not really a chalice, just a tall, ruggedly thick wine glass. There is no value in this vessel, no rare sensation in putting it to the lips.

Harry is the first who comes to take it from me. I am holding a reverent pose, watching the light and shadow slide about the surface of the thin red liquid. Harry stands there, not putting out his hands, so that I am forced to raise my eyes and look him full in the face. He is grinning. He is saying hello. He is pleased that it is me. But there is a dare at work too. And I can say only one thing to him. I am not standing here as his father. I cannot use any words I choose, or speak in any tone of voice I like.

"The Blood of Christ, Harry," I say to him.

His hand reaches up. "Oh." He shrugs and wriggles his head as he remembers he needs a formula. "Yes," he says, and takes the chalice, beyond my control, and from my step above him I can see through the glass the liquid brim against his lower lip and then swirl higher against his upper lip. I grip my linen towel in readiness. But the level subsides and Harry opens his mouth and I see a first substantial, but not excessive, ripple wash in. He reels in my eyes again to his flushed, playful face, and steps back.

The communicants pass by, perhaps one in three taking the chalice. I watch the level. It drops only slowly. I don't want to taste it again. I have had enough. No one takes it as boldly as Harry has done. I count the communicants still in the centre queue. They move forward and dwindle, and there is no one left. I stand, holding a chalice still half full. I wait, poised, but without options. From the pews, immediately in front of me, without my seeing its launch, Harry's whispered hiss bursts by my ear.

"Drink it," he says.

I turn half aside, inward to the altar, and I close my eyes and obey.